REAPER'S RHYTHM

HIDDEN: BOOK 1

CLARE DAVIDSON

Published by Smudged Ink Press

ISBN 978-0-9926113-0-9

First Paperback Edition: July 2013

For Mum, Dad, Mark and Louise.
Thank you for your unending belief and support.

ACKNOWLEDGEMENTS

Edited by Rebecca Taros Dickson
Proofread by Megan Payne
Cover illustration by Bramasta Aji and Ina Wong

Thank you to everyone who supported me while I was writing 'Reaper's Rhythm', especially Tom, Eleanor, Katy, Ruth, Sharon, Clare and Monica. Also thank you to Louise, for giving me some much needed courage.

CHAPTER ONE

The warm light seeps through the closed sitting room curtains when I step into the drive. The muffled thump of dance music grows louder as I approach the familiar front door. I push the key into the lock, but the door swings open on its own. My breath catches in my throat, but I force it into a growl. Not only has my sister, Charley, not bothered to lock the door, she hasn't latched it. Whatever she rushed home for must have been important.

I step over the threshold and a blast of warm air hits me, enveloping me like one of Mum's overprotective hugs. My wind-chilled face tingles, as I close and lock the door.

"Charley, I hope you've set the table." My voice competes with the din of the deep bass of my sister's music.

I toss my keys into the wicker basket on the hall table. As I peel my coat off, I see Charley's in a crumpled heap on the floor. Rolling my eyes, I scoop it up and hang it, then place her discarded boots in the shoe rack beside my own. Why am I the conscientious sister? I'm only sixteen. Charley will be heading off to university next year.

Stomach rumbling, I snatch up the Chinese takeout I'd picked up on the walk home and wander into the kitchen. Frowning, I flick the switch to light up the pristine room. Mum is a clean freak now that Dad doesn't live here. The table isn't set, even though Charley promised she would do it before she rushed off ahead.

"Charley," I call out and then dump the bag on the kitchen table and stomp across the hall to the sitting room, shoving the door open.

The music hits me first, making me jerk my head back, then the smell. An odd odour, metallic and rich, overpowers the air freshener on the mantel.

"Charley?" She must be trying to scare me. "Charley, stop messing around." I grit my teeth, expecting her to jump out at any second.

My body shudders and my flesh tingles as if an army of ants is marching beneath my skin. I back out of the empty sitting room and bolt upstairs. The smell is stronger, snaking down my throat, making me want to gag.

"Charley?"

I shove her door open, hard.

Charley's lying on the bed, her blond hair fanned out over the pillow. Her arms are spread wide, palms up. Crimson blood drips from deep slashes on her wrists. Her blue eyes are open, staring at the ceiling. But they don't see. They're dull, empty.

Dead.

The room spins. My stomach lurches and bile rises up my throat. I swallow and clap my hand to my mouth. Sagging against the doorframe, I can't tear my gaze from the single lock of hair resting over Charley's porcelain cheek. What should I do?

Charley would know what to do.

As I stumble down the stairs, my mind clicks into gear. A scream rips out of my throat, eclipsing the pounding music. My foot slips on the beige carpet, sending me tumbling down the remaining stairs. My shoulder and back slam against the wall. I scramble to my feet, screaming, sobbing, then stagger into the hallway, colliding into a young man with the darkest eyes I've ever seen.

My own force knocks me backwards. His strong grip clenches my arm, preventing me from falling. I try to scream again, but the sound is trapped within my constricting chest. My sister is dead. A stranger is in my house.

I writhe against his grip, lashing out with my foot. My toes crumple and sting when they hit his shin. I'm thrown off balance, but he holds me fast.

He raises his thumb to my forehead and applies gentle pressure, as he sweeps his thumb towards my brow and then hooks it back up.

"Sleep." His quiet voice acts like a sedative.

My head flops forward until my chin touches my chest. A new scent replaces the sickly metallic tang of Charley's blood: freshly cut grass. Inhaling it makes my head fuzzy and my heartbeat slow.

I want to see his face, memorise every detail. The contours of his cheeks and jaw, the shape of his nose, the colour of his hair. The police want to know those things, don't they? The only feature I can see for sure is the impossible darkness of his eyes.

My own eyelids droop, my limbs turn liquid. A strong arm loops round my back and lowers me to the floor. I fight against sleep. Each time I force my eyelids open, they flutter shut again.

"Forget," he says. The word is nothing more than a whisper at the edge of my hearing. "Sleep."

CHAPTER TWO

My eyes are closed, but I hear a soft, repetitive bleep. Where am I? Something sharp irritates the back of my right hand. My scalp itches, like my hair hasn't been washed for a week. I'm lying in a hard, uncomfortable bed, on a mattress that rustles with the slight movement of my head. Wherever I am, it stinks like an overdose of flowers. I can tell it's light because the insides of my eyelids glow red.

"Is she waking up?" Mum's voice sounds strangled. "Kim?"

"Give her some space, Cath." Dad's voice. Why's he here?

I twitch my forehead into a stiff frown. Why would Dad be here? Where am I? Prying my eyes open, I grunt through my nose. Bright morning light pours in through the large window, revealing the unfamiliar room. The top half of the walls have been painted white, the bottom half mint-green. A plastic rail runs round the walls. Dark scuff marks stain the white paint. My bed is narrow, with raised metal sides. I can see the back of a board, clipped to the end of the bed. My head and shoulders are propped up on rustling pillows. I'm covered in a white sheet and a lemon-yellow blanket. Why am I in hospital?

"Kim?" Mum's face hovers at the corner of my vision. Her eyes, normally bright as sapphires, are red and puffy. She isn't wearing any makeup and her blond hair has been hastily pulled back into a bun.

Dad approaches and leans over the other side of the bed. He grips my left hand. "Welcome back, Kimmie."

I grimace at the nickname. He knows I hate it. I try to speak, but my tongue sits in my mouth like a sanding block. I cough instead. Something tugs against my right hand. I glance down and realise why it's itching so badly. An IV protrudes from my skin. I follow the tube upwards to a clear bag of fluid. I try to speak, but only manage to croak. Dad hands me a cup of water. I sip it slowly, allowing it to soothe my sore throat.

"Why am I here?" My voice is nothing more than a weak rasp. "What happened?"

Mum and Dad exchange a glance.

Dad takes the cup from me and sets it down on the bedside cabinet. He exhales. "What do you remember, Kimmie?"

I stare at him, running my tongue over my cracked lips. My body shivers. "I was walking home with takeout." I prop myself up on my elbows, still dizzy, and gaze around the room. Flowers adorn the bedside table, the window sill, the wheeled table and even the floor. "Why won't you tell me what's happened?"

I don't think anything's broken. I don't feel any pain.

Mum massages her forehead with her thumb and forefinger while Dad dips his gaze to my blanket. Their silence terrifies me.

"How long have I been here?"

Dad lets out a long sigh. "Two days."

My eyes widen. "Two days? What happened? Where are Charley and Chris?" Knowing my sister, she's probably out shopping while I'm lying in the hospital.

Sobbing, Mum claps her hand to her mouth. She squeezes her eyes shut and shakes her head over and over. "I can't do this." She flees the room, leaving me staring at her back.

"Dad, please, tell me what's going on." My whispers quiver in the air.

He clears his throat. "Kimmie… Charley, she…" he wipes his hand over his eyes.

I clutch his hand, unable to breathe. My head spins with thoughts. "Tell me."

"Charley is gone."

I blink. Charley wouldn't leave without telling me. She wouldn't. "Gone?" My mind feels like it's been stuffed with mothballs.

Dad blows air through his clenched teeth. "She's dead, Kimmie."

My elbows give way. I crash onto the bed, staring at the ceiling. My entire body has gone numb. I don't believe it.

Dad squeezes my hand. "You found her. Do you remember?" He strokes my hand. "It must have been a terrible shock for you. I'm so sorry."

I tug my hand from his grasp. "I was walking home with takeout." The words trip out of my mouth mechanically. "Charley went ahead. She rushed off after she got a text message. She said she would set the table." Tears sting my eyes. I won't believe his words. "She can't be dead."

Dad strokes my lank hair away from my sweaty forehead. "I'm sorry, Kimmie, but she's gone."

I turn my face away from his touch. It can't be true.

"How did she seem?" Dad's voice trembles.

The IV stings my hand when I clench my fists. "She was fine. She was happy." I frown. "You know, Charley. She'd dragged me on one of her crusades."

A strained smile spreads across Dad's lips. "What was it this time?"

"Some girl at the record store sold an 18 certificate game to an under-aged kid."

"Did anything else happen? Anything at all?"

"She flipped a guy off." I can remember the crestfallen expression on that guy's face as though it was seconds ago, so why can't I remember arriving home? Why can't I remember finding my sister?

My lower lip shudders. It's true. Charley is gone. I flick my head round to stare at Dad. "How did she die?" Anger makes my voice shake. Grief makes tears collect in the back of my throat and behind my eyes.

Dad bows his head. It's only then I realise he's not bothered shaving. Salt and pepper stubble covers his strong chin and angular jaw. "Kimmie, she…" He curls his hands around the bed's guard rail, exposing the whites of his knuckles. "Charley took her own life."

My breath is forced out of my lungs in a gasp. "She was happy. She wouldn't… she was happy."

"Kimmie." He grasps my shoulders.

I struggle and scream, wrenching myself from his grip, almost tearing the IV from my hand.

"Kimmie." I've never heard Dad sound so lost and afraid.

"Charley was happy." I gulp in air, even though it stings my throat. "She would never. She wouldn't." I can't bring myself to say the words.

Dad stares at me. His shoulders are slumped, his eyes hollow. "I'm sorry." He touches his index finger to his lips. Tears gather in his eyes and drip down his cheeks. "She slit her wrists." His fingertips graze my bare arm. "Don't you remember, Kimmie? You found her."

"You keep saying that." The words explode from my lips in a scream. I flatten my palms over my face, covering my eyes. Violent sobs shake my body and choke my throat. How could I forget?

"The police think you fell down the stairs, after you found her. Shock." He pats my arm. "Maybe it's best you don't remember."

"Charley was happy," I whisper, not able to look at him.

He taps his nails against the guard rail a few times. The metallic clink makes my skin crawl. He strikes the metal bar with the palms of his hand. The force sends vibrations rippling through the bed.

"Kim, listen to me…"

I cut him off with a sharp shake of my head. "You're lying. Why are you lying?" I glare at him. "Get out. Leave me alone."

Dad steps back and wipes his hand over his chin. A sad sigh escapes him. "I'll leave you to get some rest."

My crying intensifies once he's gone. I can't control the tears.

I don't want to control them. My memories hone in on the silent news programme I'd watched while waiting for takeaway. All the senseless deaths. Stuff like that was meant to happen to other people. Not to anyone I knew. Not to my sister.

I clench my hands into fists and press them against my eyes.

Charley was happy. We'd been laughing and joking. She'd been happy.

*

The day drags by. It's impossible to keep track of the time without a clock in my room, and no watch or phone. The TV only has limited credit and I don't have a debit card to pay for more viewing time. Losing myself in mindless drivel is far more appealing than facing my muddled thoughts right now.

All I can think about is Charley. I need her to walk in the door, laughing as she tells me it's all been a joke. *"You should see your face. I should take a picture and post it on Facebook."*

She wouldn't pull such a cruel prank. None of my family would. But I still can't let myself believe she's gone.

I don't know how long I have to stay here, surrounded by constant noise. Trollies are pushed back and forth. Nurses chatter. Machinery beeps. A phone rings. Rain patters against the window. It's dark outside, but as it's the end of October, that means very little. It could be early evening or the middle of the night. I'm not sure I can stand to stay here a second longer.

Mum and Dad drift in and out. I ignore them both. I can't even look at them. How can they believe Charley would kill herself? Anger bubbles inside me, making fresh tears blossom in my eyes, robbing me of sleep. I want to sleep. Maybe when I wake up, this will all have been a horrible dream. I'll tell Charley. She'll hug me and we'll laugh about it. Please, let it be a dream.

My door opens again. My head is already turned towards the window, but I squeeze my eyes shut for good measure. Footsteps wander around my bed. A hand presses into the plastic covered mattress beside my legs. Curiosity gets the better of me. I crack one eye open a fraction just as Sophie, my best friend, hops onto the bed. She sits cross-legged, a carrier bag cradled in her lap. Her expression is solemn. Her green eyes sparkle with tears. She sniffs in an attempt to hold them back. Raindrops have collected in her caramel brown hair, which has been swept back into a ponytail. She slides her black coat off her arms and tosses it onto the armchair beside my bed.

"I didn't bring flowers," she says, gazing around the room. Her nose wrinkles. "You could start your own florist shop with this lot."

A garbled sound springs from my mouth—something caught between a laugh and a sob.

She opens the carrier bag and pulls out a pair of plastic spoons. "I brought something better than flowers."

Frowning, I take one of the spoons from her. She lifts two tubs of ice cream out of the bag.

"Don't tell the nurses," she whispers, handing me one of the tubs. She pops the lid off the second one and scoops a little of the dark brown ice-cream onto her spoon. She raises it to her mouth and then pauses, watching me intently.

The tub freezes my fingertips. I turn it round until I can see the flavour. Strawberry. My favourite. I force a smile to my lips. After flipping the lid off, I plunge my spoon in and stuff a heap into my mouth. The cold hits me before the creamy flavour. "Brain freeze," I mumble through the goop in my mouth.

Sophie eats a much more modest spoonful. We don't talk. We just eat. With every mouthful comes the realisation this couldn't possibly be a dream. Strawberry ice cream wouldn't taste so good, or so real, if I was dreaming. Tears track down my cheeks, forcing me to sniff in between mouthfuls.

"It's true, isn't it?" I ask. "Charley's dead."

Sophie squeezes my leg and gives me a small, understanding smile. My sobs grow stronger. She puts her ice-cream aside and shuffles beside me, draping her arm over my shoulders. She hugs me while I continue eating, her silence more supportive than Mum's tears.

Once I've finished, she relieves me of the empty tub and spoon but doesn't leave my side. I huddle against her, sobbing, shaking, sniffing. Safe in her arms, my eyes grow heavy and I eventually sleep.

CHAPTER THREE

Three more days go by before they let me out of hospital. A private room. The constant monitoring. No one said anything, but I think I was on suicide watch.

Dad and I don't speak during the drive to Mum's house. I'm almost relieved to get home. When I get out of the car, the first thing I notice are the neighbours' twitching curtains. I stare back, too numb to glare. The curtains drop in response.

It's odd when I walk into the house with Dad in tow. A quietness hangs in the air. I expect Charley to run down the stairs or shout to me from the kitchen. Instead, electronic music draws me towards the sitting room. Chris is cross-legged on the sofa, staring at the TV while hammering the buttons on his Xbox controller. I lean against the doorframe and stare at him. He's eleven years old and a real pain. That's how Charley would have described him. I blink moisture away from my eyes, focusing on my kid brother instead of my grief. His chocolate brown hair is currently spiked up with half a tub of gel. His eyes are completely focused on the screen.

"Hi, Chris."

He grunts in response and gives me a half-hearted wave. I haven't seen him in days—Mum wouldn't let him come to the hospital. Then again, given his overwhelmingly warm response to my homecoming, he probably didn't want to visit me.

I linger in the doorway a little longer, watching Chris's game character battering the heck out of its opponent. The match ends in a K.O. Chris remains mute while his character does a victory routine.

I wander into the kitchen. The crisp tang of disinfectant almost knocks me off my feet. I wrinkle my nose and try to breathe shallowly so I won't pass out from the fumes.

Mum is at the kitchen table, her head in her hands. Dad slips in behind me and wanders over to the counter. He lifts the kettle to check the contents, sets it down and flicks the switch.

"Chris has done nothing but play those stupid games," Mum says. "You should talk to him, Dave."

"Why don't you send him back to school?"

Mum lifts her head and stares at Dad's back. She narrows her red and puffy eyes. "It's too soon."

Dad pushes his hands down on the work surface, hunching his shoulders. He drags in a long breath. Finally, he turns round and slouches against the cupboards. "We thought you might like to say something at the funeral, Kim."

I blink and straighten my back into a rigid line. A lump forms in my throat.

Mum nods. "Maybe you could read a poem or something? I've picked a few out." She grabs a black folder that's lying on the table in front of her and opens it, revealing several loose pages. Some are printed. Others have her flowing handwriting. Receipts, lists of addresses and phone numbers, poems and readings. She tugs a couple of poems out and pushes them across the table towards me.

"I don't think I could," I say. I can barely get through ten minutes without crying.

Mum's chin quivers. She shoves the paper back into her folder.

Dad thumps two mugs down onto the worktop. "Have a think about it, Kim."

The water babbling in the kettle fills the awkward silence.

I don't intend to change my answer, but I don't want an argument either.

"I'm going upstairs," I say, but I remain frozen for a couple of seconds.

My parents don't even acknowledge I've spoken. Mum continues to flick through the papers in her folder, while Dad pours the boiling water into the mugs. It's as good a time to leave as any.

I take the first few steps two at a time but slow down when Charley's bedroom door comes into view. It's shut. Her red "keep out" sign is still hanging on the door. I edge up the final few steps and pause outside her room. Mine is the next one along. My brain tells me to keep on going, but my hand raises and knocks on her door. The silence that responds pours salt on my grief. I turn on my heel and take a couple of steps towards my own room, but something drags me back. Curiosity. Longing. I don't know, but I let my hand fall onto the door handle, push the door open and shuffle inside.

Nothing seems out of place. Mum has put fresh linen on the bed. The sash window is open a tiny crack, allowing a gentle breeze to disturb the cornflower blue curtains. A makeup bag sits on the dressing table, open with pots, tubes and brushes spilling out. A hairbrush is beside it. The sunlight bouncing off the window shimmers on loose strands of curly blond hair that have been trapped in the bristles.

I was jealous of Charley's hair. I told her once. She laughed and ran her fingers through my auburn hair. *"Seriously? I'd love to have red hair. It's far more interesting than being blond."* My shoulders shudder. More tears threaten to spill. I'm surprised I have any left.

I wobble on jelly legs to Charley's bed and flop down, perching on the edge. Dad told me she died in here. That I found her. I squeeze my eyes shut and try to remember, but my last memory is the moment I walked in the front door that night. It's like someone took a pair of scissors and chopped those ghastly minutes out.

Frowning, I bounce up and down. Then it hits me. The mattress feels wrong. It's too soft. Charley hated soft beds. I untuck the sheet. The mattress looks brand new. I shiver. I don't want to think about why the original mattress was replaced.

I dig my knuckles against the surface and push myself up. My feet take me towards the window. My gaze gets tangled up in the tree. The copper and bronze leaves have prematurely scattered to the ground, leaving the twisted branches completely bare. I shudder, but can't place why. It's not cold, but my skin prickles. I grab the curtains in my fists and tug them closed. The metal rings screech across the slender pole.

Body trembling, I lurch round, intending on escaping the room. I stop dead.

"What are you doing in here?" Mum's eyes are wild and accusing.

"I…" my voice chokes.

"Get out."

"But…"

"Get out," Mum flings her arm out, pointing to the door. "Go to your room."

I don't argue. She steps aside to let me pass. I dash past her into my own room and slam my door shut behind me.

*

A soft knock on my door disturbs my uneasy sleep. The room swims around me when I open my bleary eyes. The squat red numbers on my alarm clock tell me it's just past 9 p.m. My temples ache and my skin is tender where I've been laying on the folds of my clothes, which isn't surprising as I've been asleep for over four hours. The knock is repeated.

"Come in." I swing my legs out of bed and sit up, rubbing my eyes.

Dad slips in, shutting the door behind him. He plops himself on the bed beside me. I'm grateful when he wraps his arm over my shoulders. "I'm heading home in a sec."

I lean my head on his shoulder. His embrace holds a comforting strength, which I've missed since he and Mum split up.

"Do you have to?" I ask.

His chin knocks against my head when he nods. "Have you thought anymore about saying something at the funeral?"

I hadn't. I don't want to. I'm exhausted from grief, the long days in hospital and the questions the police asked me—questions I couldn't answer because of the gigantic gap in my memory.

"You don't have to. But I think your mum would be grateful if you did. You and Charley were close." His words are like a knife twisting in my gut.

I pull away from him. "Did she leave a note?"

Dad stares at me, his lips parted like he wants to speak but can't. We haven't talked about how Charley died since the day I woke up in the hospital.

I dip my gaze to the quilt, focusing on the red and black geometric pattern. "People who commit suicide normally leave a note."

Dad breathes in sharply. He clasps his hands in his lap. "No. No note."

"Then maybe she didn't kill herself." I stop when Dad puts his hands on my shoulders.

"Kim, the police are satisfied Charley took her own life. No evidence suggests anything else." He tucks my hair behind my ears, like he did a thousand times when I was a kid. "I understand why you don't want to believe it, but that's what happened." His voice is weary and worn.

I tug my hair back over my ear.

"You need to let this go."

I run my fingertip around the black part of the pattern, as though it was a maze.

"We all miss Charley. And I know it's hard to understand why she took her own life."

"She didn't. She wouldn't." I focus in on nothing but the quilt. I don't want anything else in the room to exist.

"She wasn't as happy as we all thought she was." Dad's voice cuts through the protective bubble I'm trying to create around myself. "Maybe the divorce hit her harder than we all thought."

I twist the quilt in my fingers.

Dad sighs. "Promise me you won't mention this again, especially not in front of your mum. Okay?"

I'd never realised how fascinating the quilt cover pattern was before. Six geometric shapes interlock in a repeating pattern, alternating between red and black. You could probably use it to hypnotise someone.

"Kim?"

I shudder, roll my shoulders back and look up in time to see his Adam's apple wobbling. The strength in his voice is not mirrored by the quivering expression on his face. I can't let it go.

I break away from Dad and cross over to my desk. I boot my computer up, tapping my fingertips against the keyboard while I wait.

"What are you doing?" Dad says.

Ignoring him, I open up an Internet browser. My home page is set to Facebook. It only takes me a second to navigate to Charley's page. I blink at the screen as I'm confronted by dozens of messages on her wall from friends: I *can't believe you're gone. OMG Charley, why? Missing you so much.* I rub the tears from my eyes and scroll past the messages, searching for Charley's last posts.

"Look," I say. "Read them. She was happy."

With a sigh, Dad stands and trudges over to me. He rests one hand on the back of my chair and the other on the desk.

"I've read them all, Kim. Over and over."

My eyes sting as I read the last message she posted, the night before she died. *Cinema tickets booked for Saturday. Treating Kim to the posh seats.*

"Don't do this to yourself," Dad says, his tone gentle. He spins my chair round, so I'm facing him.

I tuck my chin against my chest and squeeze my eyes shut. "She wouldn't have killed herself, Dad. She wouldn't. How can you believe she did?"

He sucks in a deep breath. "Because there's no other explanation. The police checked everything. Her phone. Her Facebook posts. They even searched through her school books, Kim." He rubs the bridge of his nose. "I didn't want to believe it." His eyes dance with unshed tears. "The police said it was natural to feel that way."

I shake my head, as though the action will banish his words from my mind. I slam my hands down on the arms of my chair. "Charley wouldn't kill herself."

Dad grabs me and pulls me against his chest, holding me so tightly I can't break away. I press my face against his shirt and sob into the soft fabric.

"I keep thinking it was my fault," he says, voice trembling.

I peer at him through tear drenched eyes.

"For leaving."

"Dad…"

He hugs me for a few seconds longer and then holds me at arms length. "I know it's hard to accept. It's difficult for all of us." The intensity of his stare makes me shift uncomfortably in the chair. "You can talk to me whenever you want, okay? If you want to scream, or cry, just call or come round. But please, don't talk like this in front of your mum."

I lift my head. The expression on his face melts my resistance. His brown eyes are bright with tears, his eyebrows slope upwards, slashing across his furrowed forehead. His mouth, slightly parted, waits for my response.

"Promise me?" He says, when I fail to say anything.

Turning away, I nod. "Okay."

The corners of his mouth upturn in a forced smile. He squeezes my shoulder and then stands. "Your mum and I agree you need some time to adjust to being home. With just her and Chris."

I open my mouth to object, but he cuts me off.

"I'll see you in a few days, at the funeral."

My brow crumples. "You're staying away until then?"

His eyes shimmer with tears. "Your mum thinks that's best and I agree."

"But that's not fair." I clamp my lips shut. Shouting isn't going to help anything. I take a couple of deep breaths. "You should be here, too."

"I'm not going to do anything to upset your mum."

Except breakup with her after twenty years—I still don't know why their marriage ended. A knot forms in my lungs, making breathing hard. Getting angry at Dad won't bring Charley back any more than it got my parents back together a year earlier.

"I'll see you at the funeral," he repeats. "Get some sleep." He waits until I return to my bed, before he starts to leave.

When he's halfway out the door I call him back. "Dad?"

He hovers on the hearth of my room, fidgeting with my door handle.

"I'll read something at Charley's funeral."

This time, his smile is genuine. "Thanks, Kimmie."

I don't smile. I don't think I'm capable of it right now.

Once he's gone, I flop onto my back. The mattress springs make me bounce a couple of times. I stare at the ceiling, locating patches that have become dull with age and exposure to the sun. When we were little, Charley and I would pretend there was a separate world on the ceiling. The dull patches became islands in a pure white sea. The dust motes we saw dancing in the sunlight became fairies.

I lay my clenched fists on my stomach. Charley didn't kill herself. I don't care what Mum and Dad believe—I don't even care what the police believe. My sister didn't take her own life. Somehow, I'm going to prove it.

CHAPTER FOUR

I fidget inside the black skirt suit that Mum bought while I was in hospital. The tights itch my legs. The white blouse tugs across my breasts. The skirt pinches my waist and looks frumpy.

Chris looks equally uncomfortable. He's never worn a suit in his life. It's hard enough to force him into his school uniform every morning. His mouth is scrunched up, and he's glowering at the kitchen table while Mum combs his hair out. He looks dumb with a center parting and slicked down hair.

Mum sets the comb aside and gazes at us both through watery eyes. "You both look lovely." She tugs a tissue from a box on the kitchen counter and dabs at her eyes. Her mascara is already running. "I'm going to see if the car has arrived."

The second Mum is out the door, Chris runs his fingers through his hair to spike it up.

"Much better," I say, and for once I'm serious.

He sneers at me. "You don't look so hot yourself."

He's right, I don't. It's not just the ill-fitting suit. Mum ordered me to put makeup on. I hate the stuff. Never wear it. That was Charley's thing. My eyelids are heavy with powder. Clumps of mascara flash across my vision every time I blink and lipstick smothers my lips, drying them out even more than they already were. If Charley were here, she'd have helped me do a much better job.

Chris tugs at his collar. "How long do I have to dress like a penguin for?"

I tug my suit jacket on. "Until after the reception."

He lets out a loud sigh, droops his shoulders more than necessary and rolls his eyes.

"We're doing this to say goodbye to Charley," I remind him. I breathe in to fasten the single black button. The fabric stretches and presses against my ribs.

"I'm doing this for Mum. Not my stupid, selfish sister," he says, scraping his chair across the floor and then stomping out of the kitchen.

I gawp after him. I've been so wrapped up in my own grief, I didn't realise his anger. I shove my feet into a pair of patent leather high heels and skitter after him.

Chris is pacing up and down the drive. Mum is standing on the pavement at the end of the driveway, craning her neck and wringing her hands while waiting for the funeral car. I grab Chris's shoulder and drag him back into the house. He yelps, drawing Mum's attention.

Her forehead creases. "What are you doing?"

I give her a sweet smile and kick the front door shut.

"Don't say anything like that in front of Mum," I hiss.

Chris crosses his arms and stares upwards.

"You'll break her heart if she thinks you hate Charley."

"How could I hate my perfect big sister?" Venom drips from his voice.

"Chris…"

Finally he glances at me. "She's messed everything up, Kim. Even worse than when Dad left."

I press my lips together. The lipstick makes them slippery. I can't argue with him—we've both listened to Mum crying herself to sleep every night and she still hasn't let us go back to school. The three of us are going stir crazy, cooped up in the house together and I've only been home four days.

He rubs his eyes. "I want things to go back to the way they were."

"So do I," I say, wrapping my arms around him for a hug He squirms for a few seconds, before relenting and leaning against me.

We both jump when the door opens. Chris leaps out of my embrace and slouches against the wall, casual like.

Mum regards Chris, then me. She shakes her head. "The car is here."

Refusing to even look at me, Chris tromps after Mum to the car. I hesitate. I don't want to get in that car and drive to my sister's funeral. I pinch my arm and wish myself awake. Nothing happens. I have to face reality. This is going to be the longest day of my life.

*

The slow drive goes by in silence. The limo driver has cranked the heat up, leaving me with drooping eyes and a nodding head. Anyone would think I haven't been sleeping well since Charley died. I rest my chin on my knuckles and embrace the short doze, missing the scenery that drifts sedately by.

We're not the first to arrive. A black flock of mourners hovers outside the crematorium. It's a cool, crisp day. The sky is a brilliant shade of azure. Oak trees cluster around the back of the sandstone building, their majestic leaves transformed into shades of copper, brown, bronze and gold. My gaze is drawn to the tall brick chimney dominating the grounds, making the crematorium appear lopsided. A shiver runs down my spine and nestles in the small of my back, just as Mum puts her hand there to guide me inside.

I barely register the whitewashed walls and rows of cushioned wooden chairs. Our footsteps echo on the parquet floor and scores of hushed whispers buzz around the lofty room.

An oversized photograph of Charley stands on an easel at the front. I freeze and stare at her charming smile, unable to squeeze a breath out of my lungs. I recognise the photo. It was taken the evening of her year 11 prom. She was wearing a peach ball gown with a sequined bodice that wrapped tightly around her torso. The skirt splayed out like a waterfall. Her blond curls were piled on top of her head and her makeup was expertly applied to accentuate her angular cheek bones and her full red lips. It's exactly how I remember Charley: beautiful and confident.

Mum applies pressure to my lower back, coaxing me towards the front row. Despite the cushioning, the chair is uncomfortable. The high, straight back prevents me from slouching. I jerk up to my feet when the duty minister paces in. "Angels" by Robbie Williams begins to play. Mum's choice. My lips mouth the familiar words. The bass, distorted by the poor PA system, trembles through my body.

When the song ends, I sink to my chair. My mind is numb. Charley is gone. I'm never going to see my sister again. My chin trembles.

Mum places her hand over mine. Her cool touch brings me back to the moment.

The duty minister is staring at me. "Kim? Would you like to say something?"

I fumble for the piece of paper in my jacket pocket. Unfolding it, I make my way to the microphone. The clack of my heels against the floor breaks the silence. Someone in the audience coughs. I lay the creased paper down on the podium and use my palms to flatten it out, clearing my throat.

"Remember me…" my voice crackles through the PA system. A slight whine trips me up. I stutter over the words and clear my throat again. Tears are already welling up. "Remember me when I am gone away…" My voice falters as I choke out the words to the Christina Rossetti poem. Also Mum's choice.

Tears spill from my eyes and splash onto the paper. They hit the words, smudging the ink. It looks like a dozen spiders have fallen onto the page. It's a good thing I know the poem by heart.

I pause when I reach the final couplet. Mum is crying. She keeps dabbing her panda eyes with a soggy, ragged tissue. Beside her, Chris is sitting bolt upright, his entire body rigid. He isn't crying, but his eyes sparkle more than they should. Dad, nowhere near as composed, is next. A lead weight lies in the pit of my stomach. It's horrible seeing your father cry.

I clear my throat again, buying a moment's time to scan the room. Sophie smiles at me. The small encouraging motion fails to drag my voice from my throat. My gaze wanders past her. Everyone is staring at me, waiting as though I'm the star of a freak show. I recognise every face—relatives, school friends, teachers, neighbours.

My gaze tracks back towards Sophie but stutters over the image of a young man. He's standing at the entrance, arms folded loosely across his chest. His hair, black as night, brushes his brow. In blue jeans, a white T-shirt and short sleeved black over-shirt, he definitely isn't dressed for a funeral. His dark gaze runs round the room, flickering over every member of the congregation before meeting mine. His eyes widen fractionally and then he inclines his head a little. The corners of his lips curve up and he mouths, "Go on."

The final words of the poem have flitted out of my mind. I dip my gaze. "Better by far you should forget and smile, than that you should remember and be sad." My voice breaks on the last word. I can't prevent myself from sobbing out loud. A sea of sorrowful, understanding faces swim in front of me. When I look up again, he is gone.

*

I dart down the aisle and out of the hall as soon as the service has ended. I gulp in fresh air. Mourners amble out, streaming around me. Occasionally someone squeezes my upper arm or gives me a brief hug. I break away and head to a bench in the memorial garden. The deep seat is far more comfortable than the chairs inside. Most of the autumn leaves have been swept away from the neat lawns and paths, but some stray ones litter the ground.

"Charley would have liked the service." A pretty brunette perches on the bench beside me. "Don't you think?"

I nod and smile. I know all of Charley's friends and Amy is no exception.

She clasps my hand. "I still can't believe she's gone. Can you?"

I shake my head, afraid if I speak I'll cry yet again. I'm fed up of crying.

"I liked the poem you read. Did you write it?"

I press my lips together to prevent myself from choking on laughter.

Amy doesn't seem to notice my reaction. She ploughs straight on. "We were meant to be going out the next day to the new club in town. Some of the guys thought we could go tonight, in Charley's honour. Do you want to come with us?"

I'm not sure I have the guts to sneak into a club underage. Even though I don't answer, Amy chatters on.

"Some of us are clubbing together to get a bench to put in the memorial garden at school. Do you want to chip in? Do you think your mum would?" Amy leans back and scuffs her heels against the grass. "It would have a plaque of course. So everyone would know it was dedicated to Charley. We were discussing what it should say, maybe a quote from her favourite song or something. What do you think?" She finally pauses long enough to inhale.

I shrug. "It sounds nice." I wonder who will care about a bench and a plaque in a couple of year's time, once everyone who knew Charley has left the school.

Amy squeezes my hand. "You should hang out with us when you come back to school. I know you're not in sixth form yet, but we'll look after you."

She's forgetting I have my own friends. I was never part of Charley's cohort. I didn't want to be.

"When are you coming back?"

I shrug again. I'd like to say Monday, but I'm not sure Mum is going to let it happen. She's been keeping Chris and I close, yet keeping us at arm's length at the same time. I wonder how long she can stay off work.

"There you are." Sophie leans over the bench to give me a hug before wandering round to lean against its arm.

Taking her cue to leave, Amy stands and smooths her knee-length skirt. "Think about the club? I'll call you tomorrow."

"Club?" Sophie mouths as Amy wanders away.

I leap to my feet. "Amy."

She whips round, beaming at me.

"Was Charley hanging out with anyone new before..." my voice trails off and I stare at the ground.

"No," she says. The corners of her lips upturn briefly. "Not as far as I knew. And I would have known. I was her best friend." She begins to walk away.

"Amy."

She hunches her shoulders at the sound of my voice but stops and smiles, waiting for me to carry on.

I swallow away the lump of tears forming in my throat. "Did she seem unhappy, or upset?"

A vertical crease forms between her heavily plucked eyebrows. "No. She seemed like Charley." Her chocolate brown eyes brim with tears. "I'm sorry, Kim." She sniffs loudly.

I pull a clean tissue from my pocket and hold it out. She returns to my side, plucks the tissue from my fingertips and sobs into it. At a loss for what to do, I put my hand on her shoulder and wait for her to finish crying.

She drags the tissue across her eyes, smearing her heavy eye makeup, and then blows her nose into it. "I'm sorry. I came over to cheer you up, but I'm the one getting upset." She wipes her eyes again. "Come to the club. It'll do you good to relax."

I purse my lips. Charley's friends have never shown this much interest in me. But maybe I'm all they have left of her. The breath I draw in makes my lips quiver and my chest shudder. They're my connection to Charley, too. I nod.

"Yes, I'll come."

Amy grins and strides away at a more purposeful pace.

"Club?" Sophie asks, curling her hand around my wrist. "As in nightclub? You can't."

"Kim?" Mum's call saves me from answering.

I glance round. Mum, surrounded by well-wishers, waggles her fingers in a nervous wave. She's ready to go.

"I have to go ride in the car with Mum." For me, that's "goodbye," but Sophie grips my wrist even tighter.

"Kim..."

I wrench away from her grasp. "I have to go." Normally I'd listen to her advice. Normally I wouldn't even consider doing something illegal. But right now I don't care. Amy's right. I do need to relax.

CHAPTER FIVE

The streetlights drive the darkness away from the queue waiting to get into the nightclub. I'm the youngest person here. Drizzle alights on my coat and exposed skin. My face is heavy under the weight of too much makeup, lovingly applied by Amy on the bus. I look three years older than I am but feel like a naughty kid, waiting to be caught out. She's blathering away, but I'm too cold to pay any attention. My teeth are chattering so hard it's giving me a headache.

A whole gang of Charley's friends flank us in the queue, though Amy's the only one making an effort to welcome me. It's not a fun way of spending a Saturday night, especially with the guilt of lying to Mum making me feel sick. I told her I was going to Sophie's.

Charley went to clubs before she turned eighteen at the start of September. She lied, staring Mum directly in the eye. *"I'm going to Amy's. I'll be back late. Don't wait up. Love you."* And then she vanished out the door. Sometimes, she sneaked me a wink. Was it supposed to make me feel like we were sharing a secret? I bet she laughed and joked while waiting to get in. If she were here now, she'd tell me to relax and smile. *"Enjoy yourself, Kim. No regrets, remember?"* I'm already regretting it and we're not even inside.

I'm shaking by the time we reach the front of the queue, but I can't tell if it's from the cold or fear. The bouncer towers over me—a giant of flab and muscle, dressed completely in black.

He scrutinises us both until Amy flashes him some I.D. It must be fake, because I know she isn't eighteen yet. The bouncer stabs his thumb towards the door. We obey his silent order and shuffle inside, money at the ready to pay our way in. I leave my coat in the cloakroom and slot the pink ticket into my purse.

The nightclub stinks of sweat and booze. The walls, floor and ceiling are all painted matte black. Lights flash and strobe in time to the music, which vibrates through my body and resonates against my bones. My ears pop. Every sound, except the music, is muffled. The dance floor is a thriving mass of twisting, swaying, gyrating bodies. Every inch of wall space is taken up by observers. Most are cradling drinks—bright cocktails that glow under the UV lighting seem popular—but some are tangled around partners, kissing and fondling as though they are in private. Heat rises to my cheeks and I try to avoid glancing at any of the passionate couples.

I'm in a red dress, cut just above the knee, and positively overdressed. So much skin is on show here, I wonder how everyone didn't freeze to death on the way in. But the heat inside is intense. My skin is already becoming clammy after only a few seconds.

Amy taps my arm and then makes a drinking motion with her hand. She rubs two fingers together and points at herself. I nod and Amy drifts away towards the bar, leaving me standing on my own at the edge of the dance floor.

I feel a hand on my shoulder and swing round to a grinning muscly guy. He's one of Charley's friends, although he isn't part of Amy's gaggle. Gage. He and Charley went out for a while. He took her to their year 11 prom. My cheeks flush at the thought that he's pretty good looking. His lips move but I can't make out what he's saying, so I shrug my shoulders.

He leans down. His jaw brushes against my cheek, grazing my skin with day old stubble. "You're Charley's sister, aren't you?" Even shouting right into my ear his voice is drowned out by the music.

I nod.

"What are you drinking?"

"Amy's getting me one."

Gage frowns. Amy reappears and thrusts a drink into my hand. It looks like coke. The dark brown liquid fizzes and spits.

"Looks like you're sorted." Gage grins.

"What do you want?" Amy yells.

"Just chatting," Gage says, before slipping away into the throng.

Amy glares at him until he's out of sight. "Charley wouldn't want you hanging out with him."

"Why not?" I ask. He seemed nice and Charley never said anything bad about him, even after they split up.

"She just wouldn't," Amy says. She sips her drink and begins to sway to the music.

I take a gulp of the coke. Big mistake. A burning, sour taste hits the roof of my mouth and the back of my throat. I gag, scrunching my face up. Amy bursts into a fit of giggles that leaves her wheezing and almost doubled up.

She cups a hand over her mouth. "Don't tell me you've never drunk a vodka and coke before?"

I shake my head. Has she forgotten I'm only sixteen? I shouldn't be here at all, but I'm too ashamed to leave. I stare at my feet. The floor isn't completely black. Occasional globs of chewing gum are stuck to the tacky surface. Lovely.

"I'm going to dance," Amy says, pointing towards the dance floor doing a little wiggle. "Are you coming?" I shake my head. "Hold my drink, would you?"

I tuck my purse under my arm, just as she shoves her half empty glass at me and heads off. Within seconds, she's vanished into the crowd.

I take a more cautious sip of my drink. This time, warmth fills my mouth and slides down my throat. It's pleasant for about four seconds, before the nasty aftertaste hits me.

I press my hand to my chest as Gage's voice booms in my ear. "Has Amy left you all alone?" He leans his chin on my shoulder and laughs at my expense.

I scowl and turn my face away from him.

Gage scoots round in front of me and relieves me of Amy's drink. In his other hand he's carrying a pint of dark, honey-coloured beer. He takes a sip, giving himself a frothy moustache that he licks away. He leans in to shout in my ear again. "First time in a club?"

Is it obvious? I nod and look everywhere but at him, remembering Amy's warning.

He begins to shift from foot to foot, in time to the beat. I stand stock-still and take another sip of my drink. This time, the aftertaste doesn't seem quite so bad.

"I'm sorry about Charley." His lips and eyebrows downturn when he speaks.

Curiosity gets the better of me. I wait until I hear a lull in the music, before asking, "You knew Charley well, didn't you?"

He chuckles. "I hope so. She was my girlfriend for nearly a year."

He doesn't sound bitter about their breakup, but it was several months ago.

"Was she hanging out with anyone new?" Just as I speak, the current song hits a crescendo, drowning my words.

"What?"

I clear my throat and repeat my question, shouting it so loud my throat aches. I take another sip of my drink to soothe it. Gage shakes his head and opens his mouth to speak, but an arm snakes around his neck, silencing him. A slender pair of legs wrap round his waist, as a girl hops onto his back. She clings round his neck and rests her chin on his shoulder, peering at me with cold grey eyes.

"Kim, this is Tia, my girlfriend."

Tia narrows her eyes in a look that says "and don't you forget it." I smile and wave my free hand at her. She slides off Gage's back and relieves him of Amy's drink, which she promptly downs.

"Let's go dance," she says, glaring at me, daring me to invite myself along. I don't.

"Catch you later," Gage says, allowing Tia to drag him into the throng.

Alone. Again. I shuffle back and find an empty patch of wall to lean against, in between two couples, who are so consumed with their partners, they're unlikely to notice my existence. The painted bricks are just as tacky as the floor. With nothing better to do, I carry on sipping my way through the vodka and coke, finding myself disappointed when the last drops disappear down my throat.

I push my way through to the bar and hop up onto a tall stool. The alcohol must have made me brave, because I don't even blink when I shout my order to the barman. I drop the right money onto the bar. Drink in hand, I stay where I am and survey the dancers. I catch a glimpse of Amy, rippling her body in time to the music, back to back with a guy I've never seen before. She's holding her arms above her head, her eyes are closed and her lips are parted slightly.

Gage dances into my field of vision next. His large hands are planted on Tia's hips. While he barely moves, she's wiggling in his grip. She keeps stepping forward, gyrating her hips against his groin. A stupid grin is fixed on his face. I doubt I'll ever have the nerve to dance like that with anyone.

Bored, I allow my gaze to continue drifting. The music doesn't seem so loud anymore—it's become an incessant drone in the back of my mind. My eyes have adjusted to the variable darkness, but a headache is forming thanks to the constantly flickering lighting.

A guy eases onto the stool beside me. He rests his elbow on the bar, pinching a five-pound note between his fingers as he waits for service. I find myself staring at him. Something is oddly familiar about him. His brown hair is spiked up with gel and he's wearing a shirt with a loud, swirling pattern on it. Noticing me, he raises an eyebrow. Then it clicks. I imagine him with wire-frame glasses and a blue T-shirt on. It's the guy from the record store. The one Charley was rude to the day she died. My stomach drops through my body to the floor. He gives me a nervous smile and says something, but it's lost under the roar of the music.

Straight away his attention is diverted by the barman. He shouts an order and then points at my now almost empty drink and gives the barman a thumbs-up. While the barman prepares the drinks, he exchanges his note for a larger denomination, leaving me smiling nervously. Once we both have fresh drinks in hand, he points towards the back of the room. A green fire exit sign stands out in the sea of black. I'm not sure why he wants to talk to me, but I don't feel like I can say no, especially as he's bought me a drink. I nod and follow him towards the fire exit.

When we step outside, the cold air whips into me. I start shivering instantly and wish I'd retrieved my coat from the cloakroom. To keep the cold at bay, I make a start on my third drink. The music is reduced to a pulsating beat behind the door.

"I saw the news about your sister. I'm sorry." His voice is muffled by my popped ears, but audible.

I blink, but say nothing.

"I'm Kevin." He holds his hand out to me.

I stare at it, not sure what to do. Charley was a bitch to him. Why is he being so nice to me?

Kevin's hand remains proffered for a few seconds and then he drops it to his side and wipes his palm against his jeans. "I just wanted to tell you I was sorry."

"Thanks for the drink." What a lame thing to say. I take another sip. "I'm sorry."

His eyebrows slide up his forehead. "For what?"

"Charley was mean to you. I'm sorry."

Kevin shrugs. "It wasn't your fault."

I didn't stop her. I swallow a gulp of vodka and coke, which leaves me coughing and spluttering.

Kevin steps behind me and gives me a couple of firm pats on my back. "Maybe you should slow it down a bit?"

He's right. I've never drunk before, not even wine with a

meal. I'm already feeling lightheaded and my headache is getting worse. Except the vodka is making my chest feel warm and fuzzy and, just once, I'd like to let loose and forget the hell my life has become.

"I want to make it up to you."

It's Kevin's turn to look stunned. His eyes grow wide. "Make what up to me?"

"What Charley did."

Kevin scratches his head. "Maybe we could go for coffee tomorrow?"

It sounds like a great idea, but I hesitate. "I don't want to lead you on."

He laughs. "I said coffee, not a date."

I'm not sure if his words are intended as a put down, but they feel like one. I down the remnants of my drink. "Fine. Coffee tomorrow."

"Nero's at five? I'm at work until then."

I nod, making a mental note of the time and place. An awkward silence falls between us. We're two strangers with only one thing in common: Charley.

"My friends are inside." I take a couple of steps towards the door and trip over my own feet.

Kevin catches me before I hit the deck. My glass slips from my hand and smashes on the concrete. Hundreds of shards of glass scatter out. "Maybe you should head home."

I pull myself from his arms and smooth my dress down. "I'm fine. I'm having fun." I doubt he believes me. I wouldn't.

"I'll walk you home."

I cut him off with a shake of my head. "I'll be fine." My heels scrunch on the glass as I turn my back on him and head for the fire escape.

"I'll see you tomorrow, then?"

I glance back at him and nod. Tomorrow I won't be such a bitch.

I return to the edge of the dance floor, after buying a fresh drink. The tension is draining out of my muscles. My head feels light and fuzzy. In a couple of years, I'd have been here with Charley. I can almost feel her fingertips threading through mine and the pressure of her tug, dragging me into the center of the throng of dancers. I follow, needing to please her, to be like her. I move in time with her, closing my eyes as I allow her to control my movements. The heavy beat throbs through my veins like a second, frenzied heartbeat. My body twists and sways. My arms snake above my head, one hand clutching my purse. The music wraps me in its embrace, smothering all my self-consciousness. Flashing lights bombard my closed eyes. The heat of a hundred bodies presses against my skin, coating me in a fine sheen of sweat.

I only open my eyes when the beat changes. I'm alone. Charley isn't here, but I'm so lost in the music it doesn't matter. My body follows my feet round in a slow spin. I thread my fingertips through my damp hair. Run the back of my hand against the curve of my cheek. My entire body is tingling with energy. I've never felt so alive.

My movements falter at the sight of Tia, draped against a wall beside Kevin. She catches my idle gaze and my body freezes under her stoic glare. Her lips move in sharp, snapping motions. Scowling, Kevin shakes his head and strides away. I turn my head to follow his passage out of the club. When I wrap back round to the wall, Tia is gone. Her space has been taken up by a couple, locked in a passionate kiss. His hand fondles the inside of her thigh. The pit of my stomach tingles, prompting me to shut my eyes and turn away.

I allow the energy of the dance to take control of my movements again. My hips snake, my knees bend and I dip down to the floor, before spiraling up again.

A sharp tap on my shoulder breaks the energetic spell. I pry my eyes open.

"I'm going home," Amy shouts. If our bodies weren't almost touching I wouldn't have heard her. "You should too."

I don't want to. I shake my head and twist away from her, but she ducks in front of me again.

"You're drunk," she says.

I shrug and my lips part in a girlish giggle. I'm past caring.

"You should go home." She curls her middle three fingers down and holds her hand to the side of her face. "Want me to call your mum?"

I scowl. I'm not ready to go home. Mum would freak if she knew I'd been at a club. "I'll be fine."

Amy folds her arms and tips her head to the side. If she was taller and older her no-nonsense expression might have the right effect on me. Instead, I burst into fits of laughter so violent my sides ache. It feels good. The tension coiling in my stomach explodes into confetti.

Amy grabs my upper arm, stopping my fluid movement. "It's time to go, Kim."

I wrench away from her, stumble backwards and collide with the people dancing behind me. They shove me forward, straight into Amy. She drops to the filthy black floor, crying out as her wrist takes all her weight. Guilt floods through me and I try to help her up.

She bats my hand away and struggles to her feet. "Let's go."

I shake my head. "I'm staying."

Amy scowls. "I promised you I'd look after you. Charley would want me to make sure you're okay."

"I don't need looking after." To prove it, I twist round in a slow circle, trying to lose myself in the music again.

"Kim."

I laugh in her face when she puts her hands on her hips. Her upper lip curls in disgust.

"Suit yourself," she says, before twisting and pushing through the crowd. Bodies part and close like a wave, hiding her from my view.

I should care I've pissed Amy off, but I don't. My head is warm and fuzzy. A sickly sensation has alighted in my gut. I try to ignore it. Try to become one with the rhythm again. My movements are jerky and out of time. People stare at me and laugh. The room starts to spin. My chest constricts. I have to escape.

Bodies block my path as I try to flee the dance floor. Sobs strangle my throat. The sickly feeling in my gut rises higher and higher, flooding up towards my mouth. I push with my hands and thrust with my elbows until I break free.

I don't stop running until I'm outside, gulping in the freezing air. The world swims around me, flowing in and out of focus. I slip from the curb. My heel breaks. My ankle snaps over. A sharp pain shoots up my leg. The ground rises up to meet my face.

"Easy." A pair of strong hands grab my waist.

I blink at the black tarmac, less than an inch from my face. An odd sensation of weightlessness steals my breath, before I'm upright again. I gag, wrench free of my saviour's grip and throw myself to my knees. Vomit is propelled from my mouth, leaving a bitter taste. The vodka burns worse on the way up than the way down. Sobs send me into a shaking, shivering wreck. Unable to move, I stare at the steaming puddle. I don't resist when those same strong hands take hold of my shoulders, help me stand and guide me away. Pain collects around my ankle, but I'm able to put my weight through it.

I'm led to some stone steps, where I sink down and bury my head in my hands. The tang of bile is still strong in my mouth, but my nostrils are flooded with a light and airy scent I can't quite place.

"Are you all right?"

I lower my quivering hands and come face to face with my saviour. I'm caught between gasping in surprise and throwing up all over again. It's him. The stranger from the crematorium.

"Are you alone?" Concern gleams in his eyes. His irises are so dark it's almost impossible to tell where they end and his pupils begin.

His question sends a wave of panic through me. I want to shake my head, but my neck muscles are paralysed. A little tension squeezes out of me when he cracks a smile, making me quiver. I hang on his words as he speaks.

"Why don't you call a taxi?" He glances back towards the

nightclub and nods in the direction of the bouncers. "They'll look after you until it arrives."

I reach for where my pocket would be if I was wearing my coat. A sob bursts from my lips before I can stop it. I feel like such a fool. "It's in my coat." I stare towards the nightclub and raise a shaking finger. "Inside." I don't have the energy to stand.

"I'll get it," he says, smiling.

Stomach fluttering, I pull a crumpled yellow raffle ticket out of my clutch bag and hold it out to him. He smiles again, sending a ripple of warmth through my body, and plucks the ticket from my fingers.

I rub my arms, waiting for him to come back. The paving stones have several cracks. Grass and weeds sprout up in the gaps. The darkness has washed the colour out of the street, while an amber streetlight strains to replace it. The result is an off-colour landscape that's too empty and too quiet. A couple leaves the club. They stagger past me, laughing, but don't even glance at me. I might as well be invisible.

"Here you go." He drops my coat into my waiting arms and then crouches down in front of me.

I try to force a smile to my lips, but my teeth chatter loudly instead. I struggle to fling my coat over my shoulders, before grasping the edges to tug it around me, willing warmth back into my body. I've only got a thin pair of tights covering my legs, which are now torn over my knees. Runs in the tights are creeping up over my thighs. I lift my gaze back to him, noticing he's also carrying a bottle of water.

"You were going to call a taxi." His voice—gentle and smooth like molten chocolate—prompts me to fish my phone out of my pocket.

I press the screen to unlock the phone and stare at the multitude of missed phone calls and messages from Mum, demanding to know where I am and why I'm out so late. I groan. It's almost 3 a.m. So much for a night of wanting to let go. I can only imagine how angry Mum will be in the morning. I scroll through my contacts until I find the number for a local taxi company. Mum made me save the number on the day she bought me the phone, "just in case." As I mumble the street I'm on to the weary-voiced receptionist, I'm grateful she did.

"Five minutes," the receptionist says.

I slip the phone back into my pocket.

He stands and holds out his hand. "I'll help you back to the entrance. You can wait with the bouncers."

I gaze up at him. The glow from the streetlight gathers around him, caressing his body. He's not dressed for a night-club and I don't smell a trace of alcohol or sweat on him. I grimace. I'm sure I stink and look terrible.

"I'd rather stay here," I say. I don't think I can stand.

His mouth twists into an awkward smile, but he squats down again, clasping his hands loosely.

Questions tumble in and out of my mind. Who are you? Why are you helping me? Why were you at the crematorium? None of them fall into my mouth. I can't seem to form any words at all. When I finally can force my mouth to work, I say the lamest thing ever. "I'm Kim."

He chuckles. "Nice to meet you, Kim."

That's it? I arch an eyebrow.

He hands me the water. "Sip it slowly."

I twist the pale blue cap off and follow his advice. The chilled water slides down my throat, washing away the vile aftertaste of vomit and alcohol. After several sips, the pounding in my head subsides a little.

"Keep drinking and you shouldn't feel too bad in the morning."

I screw the lid back on the bottle. If I drink any more I'll need to pee. "What's your name?"

He smiles *that* smile again. "Matthew."

A taxi pulls up opposite us. Its engine rumbles and rattles. The driver beeps the horn. Matthew stands and holds his hand out. I realise I like the sound of his name and the way it rolls around my oddly empty mind. I take his hand, allowing him to pull me to my feet. My legs wobble, but Matthew's firm arm curls around my back and keeps me upright until we reach the taxi. He tugs the back door open and supports me as I clamber inside.

I lean out. "Thank you." I want to ask him something, but the question is swimming at the edge of my memory, just out of my grasp.

Matthew's dark eyes become solemn. "You should be careful." He shuts the door before I can say a word and steps away from the taxi.

"Where to, love?" the taxi driver asks.

Stunned, I stutter through my address. I don't take my gaze off Matthew until the taxi pulls away down the street. The moment he is out of view, all the questions crash back into my mind. Who is he? Did he know Charley? Why haven't I met him before? I slump back against the seat, wondering if I'll see him again.

*

Luckily, my legs have enough strength in them to stagger from the taxi to the front door. The kitchen light is still on, which makes my stomach flip over. I try to creep past the open door, but Mum's head snaps up from where she was resting on the table.

She stares at me. "Where have you been? You weren't at Sophie's." She hisses the accusation slowly.

The weight of each word weighs me down and straps my feet to the floor. She might as well have poured concrete all over me.

"I went out with some of Charley's friends. You remember Amy?"

Mum stands and takes slow, deliberate steps towards me. "I called. I left messages."

"I know. I'm sorry." Tears well up in my eyes. My headache becomes a stabbing pain. I turn the bottle of water around in my hands.

"Anything could have happened to you." Mum stops in front of me and sniffs. "You've been drinking."

I don't deny it.

"You're only sixteen."

I flop my chin to my chest and stare at the floor.

"How could you be so irresponsible? So stupid? So selfish?"

"I just wanted to have some fun." It sounds lame.

Mum drags a sharp breath through her teeth. She waggles her finger in front of my downturned face. "Fun? Well, while you were out having fun, I was sitting here worried about you. I thought you were hurt or… or…"

Dead. I don't blame her for not being able to say it.

"I rang the hospital."

Something inside me snaps. "Charley used to go out all the time. You never sat up worrying about her."

Mum's hand streaks across my cheek. I gasp from the sudden shock of pain.

"Yes. I. Did."

I didn't know.

"I lay awake every time she went out. I couldn't close my eyes until I heard her come home."

I grind my teeth together to try to stop myself from crying. I didn't know. Mum grabs me and pulls me into an embrace. I sink my face into her shoulder. We both cry, our bodies shuddering against each other, craving for understanding and something, anything, to heal our pain.

"I'm sorry," I whisper.

Mum strokes my hair. She hasn't done that since I was eight. "I know." She pushes me back, holding me at arm's length. "Go to bed. We can talk tomorrow." She releases me, watching as I retreat from the kitchen and creep up the stairs.

I need a shower but make do with brushing my teeth. The bottle of water in my hands reminds me I need to drink. I take sips from it while I tiptoe from the bathroom to my bedroom. My curtains are still open. I set the half empty bottle aside and wander to the curtains, ready to snap them shut. I pause and peer into the darkness. My skin freezes. I swear a shadow is beneath the bare tree, but it's gone when I blink. I linger in the window for a handful of seconds before tugging the curtains shut and traipsing to my bed.

CHAPTER SIX

I'm woken up by water trickling on my head. Ice cold droplets snake over my forehead, drip down my nose and onto my lips. Flailing, I sit bolt upright. Chris can barely hold the glass of water, he's laughing so hard. The carpet is getting soaked as the contents slosh onto the floor.

"Mum said to bring you some water to help your head." He shoves the glass into my hand, grinning. "You look crap."

I set the glass down on my bedside table next to the empty plastic bottle. Then I grab my pillow and launch it at Chris. It thwacks him in the face and flops to the floor.

Laughing, Chris hightails it out of my room. "Breakfast is ready."

I rub my aching head with my fingertips before gulping the iced water Chris brought me, trying not to think about the fact his grubby little fingers were in it. The water helps. My nose crinkles as I realise how disgusting I smell. My skin is itchy with dried sweat and a stale, sweet stench clings to me. I shove my quilt aside and trudge to the bathroom, turning the shower on high. Then I peer in the mirror.

My reflection shocks me. My auburn hair is a lank grease bomb. The skin around my eyes is black with smudged mascara and bright red lipstick is smeared across my cheek. Luckily, the steam from the shower mists up the mirror, hiding the demented clown face in front of me.

The hot water hammers down on me, massaging my aching

muscles. I close my eyes and tilt my face upwards into the stream-ing water. It cleanses my skin, refreshes and rejuvenates me, lending me the strength I need to go downstairs and face Mum.

The salty smell of sizzling bacon makes my stomach flip when I walk into the kitchen. A fry-up must be Mum's idea of a joke—or torture. Chris barely manages to conceal his laugh-ter behind his hands when I sit down and sink my head onto my folded arms.

A dull smack is followed by Chris's high-pitched, "Ow!"

I lift my head long enough to stick my tongue out at him.

"And you can grow up, too," Mum says.

She slaps a plate down in front of each of us. Sausages bursting out of their charred skins, toast smothered in melted butter, pink bacon curled with crispy rind and fried eggs with deliciously wobbly yolks. I clap my hand to my mouth and push the plate away, prompting Chris to stifle a snigger by shoving sausage and egg into his mouth. The runny yellow yolk drips over his lip, onto his chin.

Sighing, mum hands him a sheet of kitchen roll. "You need to eat something, Kim. It will make you feel better." She pushes my plate back to me.

I seriously doubt it. To please her, I pick up my fork and make a show of moving my food around my plate. I even slice off a small slither of sausage.

"I think you two should go back to school soon," she says.

Chris's cutlery clinks against his plate as he drops the knife and fork. We both stare, open-mouthed at Mum. In Chris's case, it isn't a pleasant sight. I quickly avert my gaze from the half chewed bacon in his mouth.

"You've missed a lot of time already. Besides, I'm sure you're missing your friends."

I fight back the urge to nod. "Are you sure?"

Mum presses her lips into a thin line. She picks up her knife and fork and, with precise movements, slices her bacon and pops a small piece into her mouth. She doesn't look at either of us while she eats.

I pick up a slice of toast and nibble on the corner. The bread feels like sandpaper as I struggle to swallow it down. I get up and pour us all a glass of fresh orange juice. Taking a sip, I realise my choice of drink was a lousy one. My stomach twists and flips all over again.

"What about you? Will you go back to work?"

Mum's silence is all the answer I need.

"Want me to stay and keep you company?" Chris asks.

Mum narrows her eyes. "Playing pointless video games for hours on end is not keeping me company."

Glowering, Chris stuffs his mouth full of food again. His plate is already almost clear.

"That's settled. You can go back tomorrow."

Chris responds by folding half a piece of toast into his mouth. His cheeks puff out like a hamster's. Keeping my gaze on Mum, I push my plate towards Chris. He snatches it from me and gets to work on his second breakfast.

"It's an important year for you, Kim. I hope you haven't missed too much."

"I'll catch up." Coursework and exam prep are the last things on my mind. I want to track down and quiz Charley's friends. Something must have been different in the days leading up to her death.

Mum smiles, but her eyes remain dead and cold. "I'm glad you're ready to go back."

I'm more than ready.

"I'm not," Chris says.

Mum yanks my plate away from Chris and shoves it in front of me again. "Eat something."

I sigh, before obliging by dragging the fried egg onto the toast and popping the yolk with my fork. The thick liquid oozes over the bread, softening it. My stomach still doesn't welcome food, but I force it into my mouth anyway.

Big mistake.

I'm part way through chewing my third mouthful when my stomach rejects the lot. Hands clapped to my mouth, I sprint from the room to a chorus of Chris's cackling laughter and Mum's angry voice.

*

By the time I wander into the coffee shop, just before five, I'm feeling—and looking—much more human. I still have a headache, but it's reduced to a background annoyance. I've even managed to hold down some soup and bread. A quick scan round shows me Kevin hasn't arrived yet. I wonder if he even will.

I plonk myself in a brown armchair by the tall window, sinking into the thick, comfortable cushion. The shop is buzzing with chatter and the gurgling of industrial percolators. The aroma of coffee is thick and heady. I pluck a month old, tatty magazine off the windowsill and leaf through it, not really registering which Z list celebrity is on each page.

All I can think about is Charley. How am I going to prove she didn't kill herself? All I learned last night was she hadn't been hanging out with anyone new. I only know two people she pissed off—Kevin and the girl he works with. I shake the thought out of my head. The timeline doesn't track. Besides, Kevin seemed nice last night.

I reach the back page, sigh, and toss the magazine aside. I glance at my watch, 5:15 p.m. I've probably been stood up. Stretching back, I gaze out the window. Kevin is on the other side of the street, huddled up inside a Paddington Bear style duffle coat with a red scarf wrapped around his neck. Combined with his black work trousers, glasses and gelled hair, he looks like a total geek. I remind myself the only reason I'm here is because Charley was a bitch to him.

He isn't alone.

I lean forward and peer at the girl he's having an animated conversation with. Tia. She's gesticulating wildly and her face is screwed up into a mean glower. Kevin keeps shaking his head. Their lips are moving but I can't tell what they're saying— lip reading is not my forte. Tia throws her hands up and then stomps away while Kevin shoves his hands into his pockets and hunches his shoulders. He heads to the crossing, frowning.

Halfway across the road, he lifts his head and catches my stare. His expression lights up straight away and he plasters a smile on his face, too wide to be genuine. I smile back and wave my fingers at him.

He wanders into the store a minute later. "I wasn't sure you'd come."

"You're the one who's late."

He grins. "I got caught up. Drink?"

"I've got it." I motion for him to sit down. "We're here so I can apologise, remember?"

He laughs and takes the seat opposite mine, unwrapping his scarf and peeling off his coat. "Americano please." He settles back into the chair, stretching his lanky legs out into the space I vacate when I stand.

I keep glancing across at him while I'm waiting in the queue. What seemed like a good idea last night, while I was tipsy heading to drunk, now seems like a terrible one. I don't know Kevin. I doubt we have anything in common. How am I going to stretch an apology over the course of an entire drink?

I return a few minutes later with Kevin's Americano and a hot chocolate for myself. For once, I forgo the whipped cream and marshmallows. He jerks upright, scooting his legs out of my space. I settle back down, cradling the hot chocolate mug in my hands. I blow over the milky brown surface, watching the ripples as they collide with the white china.

"I really am sorry."

Kevin scratches his chin. "Like I said last night, it wasn't your fault. Besides, it's not the first time someone's been mean to me."

He sighs. "How are you doing?"

I frown into my drink.

"It can't be easy. I read about your sister in the newspaper."

"Charley didn't kill herself."

He holds his hands up. "Sorry. Sore subject. What do you want to talk about?"

I sip my hot chocolate. It's too hot and burns my lip and tongue, but I keep my expression blank so I don't look like an idiot. "How do you know Tia?"

"She's my cousin."

"You two seemed to be having a pretty heated discussion just now."

He waves my comment away. "She was just on my back about something."

I suck my lower lip in. "I met her last night. I think she hates me."

"I doubt it."

"She gave me evils because I was talking to her boyfriend."

Kevin lets out a chuckle, but it sounds anything but jovial. "She's kind of jealous." He takes a sip of coffee. "No offence, but I didn't come here to talk about my crazy cousin."

I have no idea what else to talk about. "How long have you worked at the record store?"

"And now we're onto twenty questions."

My cheeks feel embarrassingly hot. "Sorry."

This time his smile is genuine. "No worries. Part-time for a couple of years. I went full-time after I took my A-Levels last summer. I'm trying to save money so I can afford to go to uni next year."

I raise my eyebrows to feign interest. "What do you want to study?"

"Computer game design."

Figures.

"My ultimate goal is to work for Lionhead Studios."

Now I'm completely lost. I hide my ignorance by taking a long gulp of my cooling hot chocolate.

"Fable? Black and White?"

I shrug and shake my head.

"Not your thing, huh?"

I try to smile. "Sorry. My kid brother loves games though. He has an Xbox. He'd be impressed." And less bored. On the bright side, Kevin doesn't seem to be the homicidal type.

Kevin scratches his head and gives me a smile that leaves his eyes sparkling. "I'm sorry. You're really not interested in any of this, are you?"

I sit upright to pretend I am. I'm pretty sure it doesn't work. We lapse into an uncomfortable silence, sipping our drinks.

My thoughts flick back to the day Charley died. The most significant thing that happened was her stand off with the girl in the record store. I don't even know her name, but she'd been furious at Charley's accusations.

"What happened to the girl you work with? The one Charley accused of selling blood and gore video games to a 12 year old?" It was a first-person shooter game, which was only meant to be sold to people over 18. The way Charley stormed in, you'd think the girl at the store sold it to Chris.

Kevin sits up sharply. "She got sacked."

A black hole settles in my stomach. Charley wanted to be a journalist. She was always looking for a story—one that would help her into the profession, instead of having to spend three years at uni. What if her impatience got her killed?

I look everywhere but at him and twirl a lock of my hair, in an attempt to appear indifferent. "I bet she was really angry." It's not hard to recall the expression on her face. Lips pressed thin. Eyes narrowed to slits. But Charley threw her shoulders back and shrugged it off.

He leans forward onto his thighs, brow furrowed. "Kim, where are you going with this?"

"Just curious," I say, shrugging. She's the only person who'd hold enough of a grudge against Charley to hurt her. Even if the timeline doesn't fit.

"Is this about what you said earlier?" he asks. "You think Charley didn't kill herself, so you're looking for someone to blame?"

I press my hands into my lap and meet his stare. "Crazy, huh?"

"Yes."

I blink at the bluntness of his tone.

"She was sacked after Charley died. Our boss needed to watch the CCTV footage. I am really sorry about what happened to your sister, but you can't run around accusing people of murder." He gulps down the rest of his coffee. "Drink over. Apology accepted. It was nice meeting you, Kim."

I'm being dismissed. I don't blame him. He stands and I hurry to follow his lead.

"I'm sorry," I say.

He forces his mouth into a tight smile. "Do you ever stop apologising?"

I gaze at my feet. "I guess not."

He turns to leave, hesitates and glances back at me. "Maybe I'll see you around?"

I raise my eyebrows. I thought he'd be glad to escape my wild theories. "Maybe."

"What's your mobile number? I'll text you."

He pulls his phone out and taps my number in as I reel it off by rote. Nodding, he dons his coat and scarf. He gives me a final smile as he slips his hands into his pockets and ambles out of the coffee shop. I return to my chair, which no longer feels comfortable. One thing is clear—I need a new suspect.

CHAPTER SEVEN

I'm late arriving at my first lesson, thanks to a summons from the head teacher, Mr Whittaker. The class has already settled down and is taking notes off the board. Miss Granger gives me the briefest nod when I slip in and take my seat beside Sophie. The rest of the class isn't so discreet. A sea of faces stare at me, eyebrows drooped in sympathy. I curl my hands in my lap, the action hidden beneath the desk.

"Are you okay?" Sophie whispers.

Nodding, I pull my books out and begin writing the information Miss Granger has put on the board.

"You've not missed much," Sophie says. "You can borrow my book if you want."

I nod my thanks.

"We've got a history test next week." She lets out an exaggerated groan and rolls her eyes. "And we've got an assessment in English, too."

Great. Back to the grindstone straight away. Miss Granger begins talking and asking questions. For once, I keep my hand down and she doesn't pick on me to answer anything. She glances at me a couple of times, pity pooling in her eyes. I concentrate on my book.

It turns out our task is to put data from an experiment into a table and then plot it on a graph. Not useful since I was absent for the experiment. Instead, Miss Granger hands me a worksheet. Her action is accompanied by a second round of silent stares.

I bury my gaze in the worksheet. My eyes burn with held back tears. Coming back to school was supposed to be a good idea, except I feel like I'm the star attraction in a freak show. Look at Kim. Pity Kim.

"So, did you go to the nightclub with Amy?" Sophie whispers, jolting me from my thoughts.

I stare at the worksheet and doodle some answers, wondering if I'll spend the whole day treading water.

"I'll take that as a 'yes.'" Sophie touches my wrist. "How was it? Fun?" I can't decide if it's jealousy or concern hovering in her voice. I'm suffocating in concern.

"No. It was awful." Just like sitting here, pretending I'm getting on with my life. How can I, when I still need to find out what happened to Charley?

"Why? What happened?" Her touch becomes heavier against my skin.

I shake her off. "Cover me."

"What?"

I leave Sophie staring at me in bewilderment, as I scrape my stool back and dash from the room.

*

I wander through empty corridors towards the sixth form common room. It's another part of the school I've never been into, but one my entire year group fantasises about. It must be fantastic to have a space free of lower school kids. Next year, it'll be our domain.

It doesn't live up to my vision. The common room is scruffy with a bunch of tatty circular tables scattered around it. Students sit around them, playing on phones, chatting, listening to music, watching videos on laptops. Not one of them is making any pretence at working. A vending machine at one side of the room sells cans of pop, crisps and a variety of chocolate bars. The walls have been painted with garish, comic-book style murals which are too amateur to look good.

Heads rise the second I wander into the room. Amid a sea of students wearing their own trendy clothes, I'm the only one wearing the school's navy blue uniform. I fidget my weight from foot to foot, avoiding scrutinising stares while I try to find Charley's friends.

Gage and Tia are sat on a busy table—the center of attention. Beside Tia, a heavy black cello case is propped against the table.

Amy is sat a few tables away from them, laughing and joking with a bunch of girlfriends I don't recognise. Charley had more friends, just my luck they would be the ones in lessons.

My attention snaps back to Gage's table when a chair scrapes across the floor. Tia stands and saunters over to me, a smug grin on her face.

"What are you doing here?"

Now everyone really is looking at me. "I… I…" I can't force any words out. I feel like such an idiot.

Tia plants her hands on her hips, waiting for an explanation. "Well?"

"I… wanted to talk to Charley's friends. Ask them some questions. I thought some of you guys would be able to help me." Now I can speak, the words seem to be tumbling out, fast and furious. I can't stop them and it's making my face flush up to my ears. "I wanted to understand. I don't believe Charley would have killed herself."

I'm surrounded by twenty pitiful expressions. They're each so similar, the sixth formers could be wearing masks. I'm not going to get any answers from them. They think I'm losing it. Maybe I am.

Tia takes a step closer, so she's in my face. Her breath reeks of coffee and chocolate. "What do you think happened?"

I shrug. "I'm trying to find out," I say.

She huffs out a sigh. "Look, I'm really sorry for your loss, but you're not going to find any answers here. Charley killed herself. Deal with it."

"Tia." Amy is standing, but she isn't coming over. "Lay off her." Her gaze flicks to me for a second. "You should probably go, Kim."

I stay put, unwilling to be pushed out by either girl.

"Yes, Kim, off you go." Tia turns back to her table, but after a couple of steps she twists and stares at me over her shoulder. "You'd better apologise to Amy first. You did shove her to the floor on Saturday night, didn't you?"

A few murmurs rise up, words I can't hear and probably don't want to.

Amy strides up to Tia and holds up one finger. "First, I didn't get hurt." She raises another finger. "Second, it was an accident." She raises another finger. "Third, I don't need a bitch like you sticking up for me."

Screaming, Tia launches herself at Amy. Gage wrenches Tia back, hanging onto her while her arms and legs flail. Amy folds her arms and tilts her head to the side, emitting an aura of calm.

The screech of the school bell cuts through the scene. Immediately, the room begins to clear out. I'm not sure if they're desperate to get to second lesson or just glad of the excuse to leave the failed fight behind. I allow myself to be swept out of the door by the tide of teenage bodies.

I almost let myself get carried across to the main school building, except I see Matthew. I stop dead, planting my feet against the push of the crowd. Bags and shoulders bash into me. A few curses and shouts are launched at me. I ignore it all.

Matthew is standing at the corner of the main school, leaning against the wall, watching the common room entrance. I find myself wanting to see his smile, but his lips and eyebrows are tugged down in concentration. He doesn't look like a student, not even a sixth former. He isn't too old, but he doesn't fit in. Yet no one challenges him. No one even glances at him.

I pull back against the common room building, keeping my gaze fixed on him while the final trickle of students drifts past. Inside the common room, Tia's voice screeches. A second later Amy stomps out, arms still folded. She gives me the briefest glance on her way past but says nothing. I expect Tia and Gage to follow her, but they don't.

Within seconds, Matthew and I are the only ones outside. I push away from the wall and march over to him, reciting questions in my head. He turns and moves away, his stride fast and long. I have to jog to keep up, let alone close the distance. And I do want to close the distance. My shoes squish into the sports field, damp from over night rain.

I break into a run, splashing mud onto my tights and shins. I reach out. Grab his arm. Spin him round. Meet his wide, dark stare. I open my mouth. All the questions are gone.

"Don't you have a lesson to go to?" His molten voice pours over me, making me quiver.

"It can wait. I…" I want to ask a question, but it won't materialise. I take a deep breath, hoping it will clear the cobwebs from my mind, and inhale the fresh scent of cut grass in spring-time.

He raises an eyebrow, like he's waiting for me to spit words out of my mouth.

"I… you don't go to school here," I say. What a stupid thing to blurt out.

"No." He smiles.

My body melts a little. The questions have fled further from my mind. "And you didn't know Charley."

He moves his head in a slight, barely noticeable shake. He takes a half step back. I curl my arm around his wrist, holding him tight.

"But I keep seeing you. Everywhere. At the crematorium. At the nightclub. Here." Three times doesn't qualify as everywhere, but it's so hard to make my mouth form words at all.

"You should go," he says.

I grit my teeth together, ready to explode into anger if I can't get a straight response out of him. His gaze shifts past me and he inclines his head, prompting me to glance over my shoulder where I see Mr. Whittaker striding towards me.

"Kimberley Welles." His voice makes my entire body go cold.

Matthew eases his wrist from my grip. "I don't want you to get into trouble."

My mouth flaps open and closed. I'm powerless to stop him turning and walking away. This time, his stride isn't urgent. I drift back to Mr. Whittaker.

"Where were you going?" he asks.

"I wanted to know what that boy was doing on school property." I point in Matthew's vague direction, without turning to look at him.

Mr. Whittaker squints in the direction I've pointed. "What boy?"

"The one I was just talking to."

He narrows his eyes, regarding me as though I'm lying, or mad. "What boy?"

I gape and swing round. Matthew has reached the edge of the playing field. He vaults the tall wire fence easily and vanishes into the trees on the other side. No way Mr. Whittaker couldn't have seen him.

His hand curls around my shoulder. "Let's go back to my office. I'll call your mother and get her to come and pick you up. I think it was too soon for you to come back to school."

I let him steer me back to the main school building. Maybe his stare was right—maybe I am losing my mind.

*

I can see faces pressing against a classroom window when Mum arrives to collect me. I try to ignore them, but I'm pretty sure between running out of class, almost starting a fight in the sixth form block and wandering across a field after a phantom boy, a rumour has already gone round I'm nuts.

I drop into the passenger seat. "Hi."

Mum nods, slips the car into gear and pulls out of the drive. Her stare is fixed on the road. She barely even checks the mirrors. We drive along the seafront. The waves are dark and choppy. Heavy clouds obscure the mountains which squat on the other side of the bay. Moisture clings to the car windows and windscreens, making Mum flick the wipers on, even though it isn't raining.

We stop at a red light. The car engine ticks over, rumbling like an angry cat.

"I've arranged for you to see a grief counsellor." Mum's voice is so casual she could be telling me what she's made for dinner.

The light flicks to green. Mum puts her foot down a little too hard on the accelerator. The car lurches before settling into a smooth trajectory. I grit my teeth together. The car isn't the place for a conversation that will turn into a full-blown argument. I thread my fingers together and stare at the trees and houses we swish past. Every second brings us closer to home. All I can think about is the anger boiling inside me.

I start the second the front door closes behind me. "A grief counsellor?" I can't subdue my voice, the words scream out from the bottom of my lungs.

Mum treads into the kitchen and sits down. She rests her head on her hand and stares at me, hopelessness radiating from her eyes. "I think you need to talk to someone." Her voice is so calm it sets my teeth on edge. "Sit down."

I pace up and down in front of the table. "I'm fine."

"Really?" She unclips her hair, allowing her dull blond curls to tumble around her shoulders. "You claim you can't remember what happened when…"

"I can't."

Mum touches her fingertips to her lips, takes a deep breath and then carries on. "You won't accept Charley took her own life. You've been drinking."

"Once, Mum. I went out once. It was a stupid, stupid mistake."

Her shoulders start to tremble. "And today, you skipped a lesson and made up wild lies about a stranger to get out of trouble."

I open my mouth and then shut it again. I didn't lie. Did I?

"I'm worried about you." Mum's voice snaps my attention to her. She looks old. Tired. Crow's feet prowl around her eyes and her hair is dusted with strands of silver. "Go to the appointment tomorrow. For me. Please?"

My shoulders slump forward. "Fine."

"Do you want some lunch?" Mum stands, makes her way over to the cupboards and starts rooting through them. She pauses long enough to glance at me. Her mouth droops when I shake my head.

"I've got work to catch up on." I brandish my bag at her. Without waiting for a reply, I dart from the room and up the stairs.

I freeze when I enter my room. My gaze has fallen onto my bedside table and the empty water bottle. My feet are heavy, but I make them lift and move forward. I scoop up the water bottle and turn it over in my hands. It's real. Solid. Not a figment of my imagination. I hug it to my chest and sink down to the floor.

Nothing makes sense anymore. Nothing.

CHAPTER EIGHT

I'm ushered into the grief counsellor's office by a skinny receptionist, leaving Mum in the waiting room, anxiously twisting and untwisting her coat sleeve.

The office only has two high-backed armchairs, a coffee table and a full bookcase. The mocha walls are blank except for a clock—no paintings, no photos. Nothing. I sit in the empty chair and stare at Ms. Jones, my grief counsellor.

Ms. Jones is a plump, well-dressed woman. If she smiled, she might look cheerful. Everything about her is neat—from her short red hairstyle to her tidy lilac blouse, black pencil skirt and freshly polished Mary Jane shoes. A buff folder lies on her lap with a white sticky label bearing my name.

"Hello, Kimberley."

"Kim."

Ms. Jones nods, opens the folder and makes a note with a heavy pen. She tilts her head up. "What would you like to talk about?"

My brow puckers into a frown. "Aren't you meant to ask me questions?"

Her mouth twitches. "I just did."

I roll my eyes. I might as well be on some cliché American TV show. It would certainly be more entertaining if slasher music started playing and Ms. Jones turned out to be a homicidal maniac. The second hand on the clock ticks round.

I fold my arms. "I don't want to talk. I'm only here because my Mum wanted me to come." Petulance seems like the best course of action.

Ms. Jones makes another note. I shift position onto my hip and then shuffle back again. The chair cushion is too lumpy to be comfortable.

"Were you and Charlotte close?"

"Charley."

Her pen scrapes across the cream paper again.

I crane my neck to peer at what she's writing. "L-E-Y. Not L-I-E."

"Were you and Charley close?"

"Yes." I gaze at the beige carpet.

"You don't sound sure about that."

Not even a speck of dust on the carpet. I imagine Ms. Jones pulling the hoover out between patients. Or maybe she gets her scarecrow secretary to do it.

"We were." Weren't we? "We hung out together. She meant to take me to the cinema." The pressure of tears builds up behind my eyes.

"Her death came as a shock to you?"

I press my lips together. "Of course it did."

"How do you feel about the way she died?"

I begin to pick at the fabric on the arm of the chair. My fingernail works a pale green thread free. "Charley was happy."

Ms. Jones consults her file. "You found her, is that right?"

I shrug. "That's what everyone tells me."

"You don't remember?"

"The doctor at the hospital said I have a type of amnesia."

"Lacunar amnesia," she says, consulting her notes. "It's where you forget one specific event, leaving a gap in your memory."

More like a gigantic hole. I don't want to remember finding Charley, but maybe I'd recall a clue about what really happened to her.

Ms. Jones rubs her chin, right below her lower lip. "What do you hope to achieve from today?"

"I told you…"

"You're here because your mother brought you here." Ms. Jones stares at me. "I understand that, Kim, but these sessions will only help if you want them to."

Sessions. I agreed to spend one hour of my life in this woman's company, not several. I rip the green thread away from the chair and twist it around my fingertip.

"I don't want it to hurt so much anymore," I say. I heard the line in a film, or a TV show, or maybe I read it in a book. Whatever. It sounds good. Better than the truth.

Another note. "The first step to that is accepting what has happened." Ms. Jones settles back into the chair, resting her elbows on the arms. She clicks the lid back on the pen and turns it around in her fingertips. "Why don't you think Charley committed suicide?"

I slump back into my own chair. Is it that obvious? Most likely Mum fed her information.

"I told you. She was happy." I wait for Ms. Jones to say something, but all she does is watch me. "She was popular. Everyone at school liked her. She was getting good grades. She was looking forward to looking round universities."

I smother a frown by pressing my hands to my face. She was looking forward to going, she'd told me so more than once. *"I can't wait to leave this dump of a town, Kim. University is going to be a real adventure. You can visit me,"* she said when my lips tugged down into a glum expression. Which means she'd lied to me about the reason behind her crusades. She can't have been looking for a quick way into journalism. Maybe I didn't know her well at all.

"How did you both cope with your parents' separation?" Ms. Jones asks, after I lower my hands into my lap.

I scowl. "How do you think? It upset us all. We didn't see it coming." I pull the thread away from my blanched fingertip. "Charley bounced back quicker than me and Chris." Did she? Really? That was around the time she started coming home late. Was she getting drunk and chatting to strangers, or allowing boys to fondle her against the sleazy black walls of the nightclubs in town? Boys like Gage.

"You looked up to her?" Ms. Jones says. Her words are as much a statement as a question.

"Yes." She was my big sister. I idolised her.

Ms. Jones tugs a photo out from behind her piece of paper. I stare at the upside down image of Charley. It's a small version of the photo Mum chose to display at the funeral.

"You wanted to be like her?"

"Yes." I squeeze my eyes shut. Tears ooze out from the cracks between my eyelids and my cheeks. I press my palms over my eyes. My breaths come in rasps and my shoulders shudder with the force of my tears. I don't know who I am without Charley. I walked in her footsteps my whole life. I'd have been mad not to—everything came so easily to her.

I bite my lip until I get my tears under control. When I open my eyes, Ms. Jones is holding a tissue out to me. I snatch it and drag it over my damp cheeks.

She sets the folder and pen down on the coffee table, and leans forward onto her thighs. "Next time you come, what would you like to talk about?"

Has an hour gone by already? It might not have been as arduous as I thought, but I'm not sure I want to come again. I want to find out what happened to Charley, not waste my time pretending I'm accepting she killed herself. I can't say that to Ms. Jones, though. Instead, I tell her what she wants to hear.

"I'd like to talk about Charley."

*

My phone bleeps the second Mum pulls out of the car park. I glance down at the message flashed up on the screen. It's from a number I don't recognise: *Fancy a film tonight? Your choice.* Kevin. I stare at it, blinking. He really wasn't put off by my behaviour at the coffee shop.

Mum glances at me while checking her mirrors. "Is everything all right?"

"Yes."

"Will you see Ms. Jones again?"

I cover my phone screen with my hand. "Probably."

"Did it help?"

I shrug. "A little. She said it would take time." I move my head and stare at the message again. "Mum, do you mind if I go out with a friend tonight?"

She glances at me from the corners of her eyes, her mouth puckering in concern.

"To the cinema."

Her mouth softens into a smile, as she nods.

I tap the reply slot and an onscreen keyboard appears. My finger moves over the letters, swiftly typing out a brief response: That sounds good. My thumb hovers over the send button. I take a deep breath and hit it. A soft whoosh tells me the message has been sent.

"Did you talk about going back to school?"

I shake my head. "Maybe I'll try again on Monday."

"No need to rush things."

My phone bleeps again: *I'll see you there at 7?* This time I don't hesitate before sending the reply: *Sure. Looking forward to it.* I am. A night of normality is exactly what I need.

*

I wait until Mum has gone out shopping before slipping into Charley's room. It's exactly the same as the last time I was in here, before the funeral. Even though the heating is on, her room is chilly. Goose bumps break out on my arms. I don't intend to be in here for long. I open Charley's dresser drawer. Mum is predictable. I grab Charley's mobile phone and retreat to my own room.

Two phones in hand—mine and Charley's—I lay on my bed. I switch Charley's phone on. It chimes and the telecom company's logo pops onto the screen. It fades to black and a photograph of me and Charley materialises. It was taken on a rare sunny day on the promenade. We have our backs to the calm sea. Our heads, which fill the entire photo, are knocked together. I'm smiling and Charley is pursing her lips, like she's about to give someone a huge kiss.

I frown as I check her messages. I can't find the text she received the night she died. I heard it come through. Charley's message tone was the riff from her favourite song. Whatever the text said, it's gone. I doubt the police would have deleted it. Charley must have. But why?

The most recent message is one from Mum. *Running late. Chris at Dad's. Get takeout.* We both received it. We were chatting about nothing in particular. Charley was smiling and laughing, her arm looped through mine. When our message tones went off at the same time, the laughter stopped. We read the text and exchanged a weary glance. Charley's shoulders slumped. *"I vote Chinese,"* she said, splashing a smile across her face in an attempt to cheer us both up. *"We had Indian last night."* Her eyes sparkled. *"Or at least you did,"* she said, poking me playfully in the stomach and grinning.

It feels like a lifetime ago, not a few days.

I press the phone icon and an alphabetical list of her contacts comes up.

One by one, I read numbers from her phone and punch them into my own. Every time, I hear a pop and then the soft ring tone.

"Hello?" The voice that answers always sounds uncertain. Charley's friends don't know my number.

"Hi. It's Kim… Charley's sister."

"Oh, hi." They're never pleased to find out it's me, but they hold on all the same, waiting for me to say something.

It's easier to pluck up courage when I'm not face to face with a room full of sixth formers staring at me. "I wanted to ask you a couple of questions about Charley, if it's okay?"

I hold my breath through the inevitable pause. "Yeah, sure."

Let the breath escape my lungs so I can squeeze the question out. "Was she hanging out with anyone new before…" I can't make myself say the next words. I don't need to. They know what I'm trying to say.

Another pause. "No. I don't think so." The answer is the same every time.

"Was she… okay? Was she acting like normal?"

This time the answer comes quickly. "Yes. I'm really sorry. Her death was a real shock. I don't know how you must be feeling."

The barrage of sympathy makes me want to hang up, but I hold on a moment longer. "Thank you."

"Anything else?"

"No. Bye."

The line goes dead without any further response.

I sigh and look for the next number to punch in and repeat the whole process again. I skip past Amy's number. I've already spoken to her, asked my question and received the same answer. Charley doesn't have Tia's number. It doesn't matter. I don't want to speak to her, either. Gage's is missing too. She probably deleted it when they broke up.

After fifteen phone calls I drop both phones onto the bed. I haven't exhausted Charley's phone book, but my energy is depleted. My voice became strained and cracked with every passing phone call. My stomach tied itself into knots every time the answers were the same.

Charley was happy. She hadn't made any new friends.

My eyes drift shut, only to snap open two seconds later when I hear a rap on the door.

"Kim?" Mum pushes the door open a fraction and peers inside. "Are you all right?"

My hand drifts over Charley's phone, concealing it. "I'm fine."

Mum pulls her head back in response to the edge in my voice. "Dinner's ready. I made it early because you said you were going out tonight."

I push myself up onto my elbows. "Thanks."

"Is Sophie coming here first?"

I shake my head. "I'm not going with Sophie. I'm going with Kevin." Big mistake.

Mum's forehead creases and her mouth becomes small. "Is he a school friend?"

I hesitate, running my fingers round the rim of my phone. "Yes." It's easier to lie than answer any more questions. I never used to lie to Mum.

She lifts her gaze again and stares at me for several seconds. Finally she nods. "I made your favourite. Lasagne. I'll see you downstairs."

My elbows shudder and give way the second Mum is out of the room. I stare at the ceiling, my chest tightening. Does she know I was lying? My phone rings, the incessant drone shoving my guilt temporarily out of my mind.

"Hi, Sophie."

"Hi yourself." There's a brief pause and an intake of breath. "Are you okay?"

"Yes." I stare at the ceiling. "I bet the school is rife with gossip about me."

Her silence proves my theory. I sigh.

"Want me to come over tonight?"

"No." I almost tell her about Kevin and the cinema, but she'd jump to conclusions. "I'm tired. Maybe tomorrow?" Now I'm lying to my best friend, too.

"Sure, I'll see you then. Bye." Her voice is bright.

I mumble a goodbye and hang up the phone. What's happening to me?

*

By the time Kevin and I leave the cinema, I'm feeling lighter. I chose a comedy and spent most of the film with my sides hurting with laughter. We step into the foyer, which is packed with people queuing and others, like us, meandering before leaving.

Kevin is wearing contacts instead of glasses. He's dressed casually but in far more muted colours than he wore to the night-club. I can't say I'm not glad. He pinches some popcorn from my almost empty carton. I half-heartedly try to backhand him across the arm, but he slides away grinning. I find myself laughing. Tension flies away from my shoulders and neck. We stop just outside the glass doors. A genuine smile creeps across my lips.

"Thanks. I had a great time tonight," I say.

"It doesn't have to end now. We could go for a drink."

I give him a sheepish smile. "I'm underage, remember?" Tension creeps back in, weighing down my shoulders.

His lips scrunch as he chews the inside of his cheek. "Maybe we can get a coffee again at some point?"

I take a half step back. "Kevin…"

He holds his hands up, palms facing me. "Just friends. I know, Kim. I'm not expecting anything else."

Neither of us closes the gap I opened. We stand in awkward silence, while I scuff the toe of my shoe against a pink glob of old chewing gum stuck to the concrete.

"Do you want a lift home?"

My first instinct is to say no, even though it's dark and cold. The alleyway is completely undercover, but the heavy patter of rain drones at either end. Water smashes against the pavement. I huddle into my jacket and nod.

"It's this way." He heads right.

We've barely taken two steps when a couple burst into the covered alleyway, holding their coats over their heads. Laughing, they slow to a stroll and lower their coats, revealing their faces. A groan escapes me. Tia sees me at almost exactly the same moment.

Ignoring me, Tia approaches Kevin and hugs him.

"You should have told us you were going to the cinema, we could have double-dated," she says. The corners of her lips hitch into a smile.

"Maybe next time," Kevin replies. "We'd better go." He turns to leave.

Before I can follow him, Tia curls her hand around my wrist and whispers in my ear. "You'd better not be leading my cousin on."

"Come on, Tia. We'll miss our film." Gage tugs at her arm.

She releases me and in a louder voice says, "Have fun, you two."

I smile, determined not to let her get to me. I've no idea what I've done to make her so hostile.

A burst of activity at the other end of the alleyway catches Tia's attention. Amy and a gaggle of girls are wandering towards the cinema entrance. Amy's nose scrunches into a frown when she sees us.

Tia uses the back of her hand to smack Gage lightly across his chest. "Let's go."

Gage shoots me a smile. I don't return it, but I do watch their backs while they saunter into the cinema and join the queue.

I offer Amy a wave as she approaches, but she turns her face away from me. I sigh. A lift seems like a great idea. The sooner I get home, the better.

"What did Tia say to you?" Kevin asks, once we're alone in the alleyway again.

I shrug. "You offered me a lift?"

"Sure."

We've barely reached the end of the alleyway when my phone beeps. I hover in the dry. Stray splatters of water splash against my face as I check the message on my phone: *You've been asking the wrong questions about Charley. It's who she stopped hanging out with that matters. Meet me tomorrow after school. Amy.*

CHAPTER NINE

Cars zip past, streaming through the junction before the lights turn red. I lean against the wall of an estate agent. The traffic in both lanes grinds to a halt. The fumes from the car exhausts tickle my nose, making me sneeze. Between them and impatient drivers revving their cars, my head is starting to pound. I alternate between checking the time on my phone and reading Amy's message. It makes no sense to me. Charley hadn't mentioned falling out with any of her friends recently. The cars roll forward again, picking up speed. I shiver inside my padded coat. The days have stopped trying to be warm as the days plod into winter.

On the other side of the road, Amy wanders up to the crossing. Her brown hair is pulled back into a ponytail, showing off ear buds and a trailing white wire vanishing inside her grey woollen coat. I smile and wave. My heart sinks when she returns my gesture with the briefest of finger waggles. Her shoulders are jogging to whatever music she's listening to. Smiling, her eyelids close.

A rich, metallic tang fills the air. My nose wrinkles. My forehead crumples. Something is familiar about the depth of the scent and the way it coils down my throat to prowl around my stomach. I can't place it.

Amy steps forward.

Brakes screech.

Her body lifts. Falls. Smashes onto the car's bonnet. Bones

crunch. Metal crumples. Glass cracks and scatters. Her body smacks to the ground.

A scream fills the air. The way my throat hurts it must be me making the inhuman wail, but I'm too detached to stop.

The driver of the red car is sitting behind the wheel, screaming, sobbing. Music blares out of the open window, a heavy, heady dance beat skulks through my body and invades my mind. My feet carry me towards the road and the single row of moving traffic. Each driver who passes glances at Amy's crumpled form and the crowd gathering round her. They aren't paying attention to the road in front of them. They aren't paying attention to me as I reach the edge of the pavement.

"Stop." A smooth voice fills my head. The music is pushed out of my mind, smothering my desire to go forward. "Step back."

My body jerks backwards away from the road.

"Again."

I obey.

"Again."

I take a third step back, each movement taking me a few inches further from the terrible scene. But I can't lift my stare from Amy. She's laying face down, one arm twisted awkwardly. The asphalt is slick with her thick blood.

"Again."

A man stuffs his phone into his pocket and kneels down beside Amy. The blood soaks into his black trousers, but he doesn't seem to care.

A hand cups around my elbow. "Kim. Come with me. Now."

It's Matthew.

The fresh scent of spring explodes around me, pushing away the sickly metallic stench invading every pore of my body. My feet are rooted to the spot. His touch feels real. His voice beside my ear feels real.

"I need you to come with me." His voice is laced with urgency. "Now."

The music, rising to a feverish crescendo, explodes back

into my mind. My ears pop, buzz and ache. My head pounds. "Amy…" I try to step forward.

Matthew's firm grip holds me back. "You can't do anything."

I blink away the blinding tears. "She must be scared. She must be…"

The red car's engine shudders and dies, causing the invasive music to flatline.

Matthew swings me round and slips a finger beneath my chin, forcing me to look up. I meet his solemn dark gaze and it tells me everything words cannot. Amy is dead. My legs buckle beneath me.

"Don't faint." Matthew wraps an arm around my back, forbidding me to fall. "Come with me. Please?"

Sirens wail in the distance, edging closer through the traffic. "Please?"

The sickly stench creeps back up my nose. The beat's ghost still thrums within my body. My head becomes heavy. I tug away, angling my body towards the traffic, which is slowly pouring round the corner opposite us.

Matthew yanks me back. "We have to go."

I don't want to. Charley is dead. Amy is dead. What's the point?

And then he smiles, its magnetism stronger than my morbid desire. He pulls me away. I'm too exhausted to resist.

*

I'm barely aware of the walk, because my mind and body are so numb. The only thing I can truly feel is Matthew's hand cradling the small of my back, guiding me. The foul metallic stench slowly evaporates from my body, replaced by a freshness that makes me giddy.

He leads me to a playground. Even though the sun is setting, it's busy. Yet the moment we arrive, parents start calling to their children and it gradually empties out. I sink down onto a swing and wrap my arms around the chains. My body sways back and forth slowly.

"She walked straight into the road," I whisper. My eyes

won't focus on anything. I tilt my head until it rests against the cold, hard chain. "Why would she do that?"

"I'm sorry." Matthew comes into sharp focus. He's sitting opposite me on a bench, hands loosely clasped between his knees. His eyebrows tilt upward towards the center of his forehead. His eyes are large. His gaze searches mine, but I'm not sure what he's hoping to find.

I mean to respond with a question, but mothballs pack my brain, stopping me from thinking. My face becomes taut. Frustration builds up within me, rising from the pit of my stomach, bubbling up through my chest. It explodes from my mouth in a scream.

"Why can't I think when I'm around you?"

He lowers his head and stares at the ground, his shoulders stiff, back rigid.

I push myself from the swing, ignoring the whine of the hinges. I stride over to him, repeating the same word over and over, "Why? Why? Why?" I'm shouting by the time I reach him.

Matthew lifts his head, meeting my angry stare. I lurch to a stop. His hand snaps out, fingers curling over the crown of my head. His thumb presses against my forehead, sweeping right to left in a shallow arc. He repeats the action as a mirror image, before tracing a small semicircle.

"Clarity," he says in a commanding tone.

The word explodes through my mind like a bolt of lightning. I stagger back, stumbling to the ground. I land hard on my hip, but bite down a yelp. Matthew's entire body sags. The colour drains out of his cheeks. The sparkle in his eyes fades, leaving me staring at a pair of dull discs. All the questions I have ever wanted to ask him cascade into my mind and rush into my mouth. I clamp my teeth together, almost biting my tongue, to prevent them all tumbling out in one long tirade.

"What did you do?"

He runs a hand over his face. "I made it possible for you to think around me. It's what you wanted, isn't it?"

His words don't make sense, but nothing about him does. Whatever he's done, he looks exhausted.

He attempts a smile, but his lips barely move. He looks up and then glances over his shoulder. We're alone.

I can't keep the questions in any longer. I fire them at him. "Who are you? Why were you at the crematorium? Why couldn't anyone see you at school? Why did you help me? What's going on? Why did Amy walk in front of the car? What happened to Charley?"

As each question slams into him, Matthew pushes himself further back against the bench. He raises his hands, but if he's trying to shield himself, he's wasting his time.

The last question chokes my voice. Everything comes crashing down on me: Charley. Amy. Grief. Anger. Hatred. Tia. Gage. Guilt. Kevin. I tilt my face skywards and scream. Then I cry. Sobs break free as strangled coughs. My chest constricts. My breath rasps in my throat. My stomach heaves, making me dry-retch. I stare at Matthew through tear-soaked eyes. I long to be held, comforted. I long to see his smile. But he doesn't move. And he doesn't look at me. His face is so void of compassion, it makes me want to scream. It's hard to imagine he's the same person who gave me encouragement at Charley's funeral, or who looked after me when I was drunk.

Shaking, I stagger to my feet and close the distance between us. "Who are you?" I practically spit the question in his face.

He finally looks at me. "You wouldn't believe me if I told you." His voice is unnervingly calm. I open my mouth, but he cuts me off. "Kim, I need you to promise me something."

My skin prickles. My body tenses. He wants me to promise him something? This walking enigma who made me think I was going insane?

"What right do you have to ask me to do anything for you?"

"None."

I'm drawn to his eyes. I could fall into those pools of darkness and never resurface. I shake myself and lower my gaze.

I don't want to fall under his spell. Thank God he doesn't break out his smile.

"What do you want?" My mumbled words are barely audible.

"Stop trying to find out what happened to your sister."

I can only think of one reason he'd want me to back off. He must be involved somehow. Horror wrenches my stomach. How does he know I've been trying to find out how she died?

"You've been following me? Watching me?" I step away from him.

My explanation is the only rational one. It's why he was at the crematorium, the nightclub and school. It's why he was there today when Amy walked into the road. It's why he isn't denying my accusation.

I narrow my eyes. "Why are you sorry?"

He stands, but for every step he takes towards me, I take three away from him.

His shoulders slump. "I checked on you, to make sure you were all right, but I haven't been following you."

He's lying.

"Why. Are. You. Sorry?"

The backs of my knees hit the swing. I slip around it, grabbing the seat and pulling it back. I hold it primed, ready to launch it at him if I need to.

"Because I didn't get there in time to save your friend. I'm sorry."

"Save her?" My fingers ache and tremble.

He doesn't respond. It's as though he's letting me work it out for myself.

"Like you saved me?"

He's as still as a statue. Staring. Waiting. Hoping.

I realise it's true. I would have walked straight in front of a car, just like Amy did.

"I heard your voice in my head." I make myself match his stare, but fight against the lure of his eyes. "How is it possible?" My body quivers.

He doesn't respond.

I snort. I'm not sure why I expected him to. Amy's text pops into my mind.

"I'm not asking the right question."

That gets a response. His brow furrows.

My grip tightens on the swing seat. "*What* are you?"

It's his turn to back off, but he doesn't move fast enough. I push the swing with all my might. It collides into his chest, knocking him off balance. Instead of running, I launch myself at him, barrelling into him.

The safe play surface absorbs the impact as we crash onto the ground. I sit on his chest, pressing my hands against his shoulders in an attempt to hold him down. Tears spring into my eyes again.

"What are you?"

He catches hold of my wrists, twists his shoulder and pushes with his foot, dislodging the precarious combination of our entwined bodies. We roll over and I'm pinned to the ground. His grip on my wrists is so gentle I can almost fool myself into thinking I can writhe free, that I still have some control over the situation.

He lowers his face so our noses are a hair's breadth apart. I can't avoid his gaze, short of shutting my eyes. Even though my body is pressed against the ground, it feels like I'm falling through the endless darkness of his eyes. My breathing becomes fast and shallow. My heart races in my chest. The rush of blood thunders in my ears.

"Stop trying to find out what happened to Charley." He's not asking anymore. "You have no idea what you're messing with."

"And I suppose you do?" My words sound brave, even though I'm trembling like a leaf.

His body is completely still. "Two people have already died." He dips his head, leaving me staring at his jet-black hair. The ground becomes solid against me, catching me as his eyes release me. When he lifts his head, he's careful not to make eye contact with me. His expression is earnest.

"I'm not following you, Kim. I'm trying to find out who's responsible for your sister's death. I can't guarantee I'll be close if they make an attempt on your life again."

My chin trembles. "They?"

He releases my wrists, skitters away from me and stands in one action. "Let it go. I promise you, I'll find out who killed her."

I choke out a laugh as I stand. "You're what? Eighteen? Nineteen? You're not the police."

Matthew narrows his eyes. "If you ignore my warning, I will not be responsible if anything does happen to you." He strides away.

"Tell me what's going on."

His only response to my scream is to break into a run. He vaults the playground fence and sprints away from me.

*

Sophie is waiting for me in the kitchen when I get home. From her glassy-eyed expression, it's obvious Mum has been chatting to her non-stop. Probably about me. She gives me a cross stare, as I enter, which vanishes when her mouth drops open a fraction.

"Let's go upstairs. I've got some class notes and homework to give you," she says, standing before Mum can quiz me about where I've been. She tugs me out of the kitchen. One of the things I love about Sophie is her whirlwind personality.

She waits until I've collapsed onto my bed before saying a word. "What's wrong?"

I don't speak. Amy is dead.

Sophie sits beside me and guides my head onto her shoulder, hugging me as I start to cry all over again. I can't shake the image of Amy out of my mind.

"It's okay," Sophie whispers.

It isn't okay. How can it be? Two people are dead.

"Give it time. It'll hurt a little less."

She thinks I'm upset about Charley. She doesn't know what's happened to Amy. Even if my tears were because of Charley,

I'm not sure I want to feel less pain. Will it mean my love for her has faded? But I can't keep feeling this raw and weary.

Sophie rubs my back between my shoulder blades. "How did the visit to the counsellor go?"

"It's not that," I mumble.

"Then what is it?"

I could tell her about Amy. Sophie's my best friend, I can tell her anything. I open my mouth, but the words drown in my throat. If Matthew is to be believed, Amy was murdered. I can't drag Sophie into the nightmare I've trapped myself in. If anything happened to her, I'd hate myself. I can't tell her. I press my face harder against her shoulder, as my body lurches with the force of my sobs. Who can I talk to? Who can help me?

CHAPTER TEN

I clap my gloved hands together and stamp my feet. My breath puffs out in miniature white clouds, which disperse into the chill air. I should go into the police station. Inside, two officers sit behind a high desk, chatting and laughing.

It's almost a day since Amy died. As far as the city is concerned, it's a normal Wednesday.

I saw her last night, in my dreams. Watched her body arc through the air and flop down like a broken ragdoll. Stood by while her blood flowed from her body. You can't do anything.

"Are you all right?"

My head snaps up in answer to the question. I lock gazes with a policeman, his kind eyes hooded by drawn down eyebrows. One officer is left alone behind the desk—a woman peering out through the glass at me.

"Y-yes." My stammer betrays me.

"Did you want to come in?" He indicates towards the door of the station, which is slightly ajar, allowing the precious heat to spill out.

I should go inside. "No. I'm just waiting for a friend." I glance at my watch and force a grin to my lips. "He's late."

The policeman's broad shoulders stiffen beneath the thick black fabric of his jacket. "If you're sure…"

I tug the corners of my mouth even higher. The smile probably looks ridiculously fake. "I'm sure." I pull my phone out of my pocket. "I'll text him and tell him to meet me in a coffee shop. It's freezing out here." I stare at the screen of my phone, willing the policeman to go away.

He stands his ground. "Sometimes people are scared about coming in and chatting to us. You don't need to be."

My clumsy thumb slides over the onscreen keyboard, typing the message I assured him I'd send. He lifts his chin a little, observing my every move.

"Done." I grin at him. "Sorry for worrying you." I turn forty-five degrees and march away. Even though I want to, I don't look over my shoulder.

My phone bleeps in my pocket, telling me I've received a reply to my text: *Working, sorry. Drop by the store? Kevin.* My stomach sinks. I hadn't even realised who I'd sent the text to. What must Kevin think? I'm interested, despite what I said at the cinema? I shove my phone into my pocket but keep my hand nestled inside, embracing the handset.

I round the corner, stop and flop against a cream stone wall. Maybe I should have gone in and told the police I'd witnessed Amy's *accident*. I shake my head. Plenty of people were present. They would have given statements. What else could I say? Some mysterious guy thinks Amy was murdered? Scrap that. Matthew isn't mysterious. He's weird. Unsettling. Scary. I can't go to the police.

I run my thumb over the sleeping phone screen. I can go to normal, geeky, boring Kevin.

*

I don't pay any attention to the CDs I'm leafing through in the bargain bucket. Kevin is busy at the till. I didn't know the store would be so full during work and school hours. I flick the CDs back into place and wander round to the chart section. I scan the covers in the top twenty. If asked, I wouldn't be able to recall a single title or band.

A tap on my shoulder makes me leap out of my daze.

"Are you okay?" Kevin asks, his voice every inch as concerned as the policeman's.

I'm getting bored of hearing the same question. My chin

trembles. I suck my lower lip in and shake my head. "Amy…"

"I know. I heard."

I'm not sure what else to say. It's obvious he doesn't either, by the way he stands, scratching the back of his neck. My vision begins to blur with tears.

"Adam, I'm taking my break," Kevin says, placing his fingertips against my shoulder blade. "Come on."

He leads me through a staff only door, down a cold corridor with bare plaster walls, into a dismal staffroom. A stand heater in the corner pumps out heat, making the windowless room stuffy enough to cause my nose to run. A rank scent hangs in the air and it doesn't take long for me to work out why—a couple of pairs of filthy running shoes are discarded on the floor beneath the coat rack. A kettle and a microwave sit on a cheap MDF table. The microwave door hangs open, revealing the interior which is spattered with red, yellow and brown, reminding me of a piece of modern art.

"Sorry about the mess." Kevin motions for me to sit down on one of the threadbare armless seats.

Wrinkling my nose, I obey, only to discover the cushion is deceptively plump. The foam pad has been so badly compacted the springs poke up and dig into my bum and thighs. I shuffle about but fail to find a comfortable way to sit.

"Am I allowed in here?" I ask.

He shrugs. "Adam won't mind."

He tugs an orange plastic chair in front of my seat, sits down and leans forward onto his thighs. He gives me a slight smile. I find the way his glasses magnify his eyes distracting.

"Did you know Amy?" I ask.

He waves my question away. "Only vaguely, through Tia. I didn't know you and Amy were close?" His eyebrows rise slightly on the final word.

I sniff. "We weren't." I glance around for a tissue, but can't see any.

"But she was Charley's friend? Is that it?"

I cough in an effort not to cry, but the sobs take over anyway.

I press my palms over my eyes. The springs in the chair beside me creak. The heel of Kevin's hand makes circles on my back. I accept the comfort, even though I know I probably shouldn't.I couldn't confide in Sophie and she's my best friend. But I have to talk to someone. I can't keep it all trapped inside.

"I was there." I blurt out in a series of coughs and croaks.

Kevin stops massaging my back but doesn't lift his hand away. "You were there?" His voice is quiet.

I nod. "When she… when the car…" I lower my hands and stare at Kevin. "She just stepped into the road."

Kevin's hand slides from my back. "I'm sorry."

"It's not your fault." I brush my tears away. Kevin and the room still look blurry.

"It must have been horrible."

All I can do is nod and sniff loudly. I need a tissue so badly I'm tempted to use my sleeve.

Kevin cups my hand between his. "I really am sorry, Kim." He drops my hand, stands and begins to pace up and down the length of the room. "No one should have to see something so horrible. And so soon after Charley…" He stops and stares at me. "You must be sick of the police."

"I didn't speak to the police."

His eyes grow wide. "But if you were a witness, I thought you'd have to."

I open my mouth and then shut it again, unsure what to say. I feel crazy, like when I was standing outside the police station.

"Kim?"

"A friend showed up and took me home in the confusion." The lie tumbles out of my mouth in a muddle of stammers. "It was busy. Lots of other people saw what happened." I stare at the floor.

The carpet is old and stained with splashes of dark brown and faded red. Coffee and blackcurrant, possibly wine. Yet Amy's broken body flashes into my mind and the red stains warp into the shape of her pool of blood on the road. My body convulses in a violent shudder.

"Which friend?" Kevin's voice is casual, but his stance is tense.

I frown at the question, unsure what to say or why he's interested. "You don't know her."

We both look toward the door when it bangs open.

Adam hovers in the doorway. "Break's over, Kevin. Back onto the floor."

"Sure. I'll be there in a sec."

Adam glares at me and then backs out of the room.

"I have to go." Kevin almost sounds relieved.

I drag my hands over my face again. I must look awful with tear soaked cheeks and snot dripping from my nose. I wander over to the sink, turn on the tap and cup my hands beneath the tumble of cold water. I splash it over my face, shivering as droplets slide round my jaw, down my neck and beneath my jumper and T-shirt.

I turn round, leaning against the counter. "Thanks for the chat."

Kevin stuffs his hands into the pockets of his black trousers. "I'm not sure I was much help. Come on, I'll show you out."

I head towards the door, stopping when Kevin intercepts me and puts a hand on my arm.

"I'm sorry you've had such a crap time recently, Kim."

I stare at his hand, looped around my wrist. The light, wariness of his touch tickles my skin. The moment of contact lasts a little too long, before he snatches his hand away.

"I'm sorry," he mumbles, before I head out the door.

CHAPTER ELEVEN

I dump my bag down in my room at Dad's house. Something doesn't look right, but it takes my foggy mind a moment to work out what's wrong. When it does, my breath escapes my body in a sharp hiss.

Charley's bed is gone. So are her chest of drawers and wardrobe.

I curl my hands into fists. The stark contrast pierces my heart. Mum has kept Charley's room exactly the same, while Dad has erased all memory of her.

My feet pound down the stairs. I burst into the sitting room and open my mouth to shout at Dad. No sound comes out. He's sitting on the brown leather sofa, staring at a photo. I edge round the room until I'm standing behind him. It's a copy of the photo that hangs in Mum's hallway—the last school photo of me, Chris and Charley. A lump sticks in my throat.

Dad sets the photo aside and angles his body so he can face me. "Sorry, Kimmy. You've come here for a break." The sparkle in his eyes betrays his unspoken words. He doesn't want me to see him cry.

I lean over the back of the sofa and wrap my arms around his neck, hugging him tightly.

He curls his hands around my arms. "Thank you."

It must have been hard for Dad, not having anyone to grieve with. I bite my lower lip. "I'm sorry. I should have come to stay with you sooner."

Dad squeezes my arm. He doesn't need to say a word. He understands.

The sharp ring of the doorbell interrupts our father-daughter moment. Dad disentangles himself from my embrace. "I ordered takeout. I hope pizza is okay."

While he heads to the door to pay, I wander into the kitchen and set the table. At least, I put out a roll of kitchen towel and a couple of side plates.

Dad plops the box onto the center of the table and opens the lid. Warm steam fills the air, carrying the delicious scent of melted mozzarella, pepperoni and ham.

"Tuck in."

I don't need to be told twice. We both grab a slice. I sink my teeth into mine. The cheese is not quite hot enough to burn the roof of my mouth. Juicy fat dribbles into my mouth and slides down my throat, melting the lump forming there. I grab a sheet of kitchen towel with my spare hand, holding it ready to dab the corners of my mouth and my lips, which are glossy with pizza juice.

"How are you doing?" Dad asks.

I make him wait while I finish my first slice.

"Your mum said you didn't have a great time when you tried to go back to school."

I roll my eyes. "Did she also tell you she's making me see a shrink?"

"A grievance counsellor." Dad leans back in his chair and loops one arm over the back. "I think it's a good idea."

I screw my mouth up and scoop up another slice. I waste no time in devouring it. Dad shows a greater sense of decorum, taking leisurely bites out of his own slice.

"I heard about Charley's friend, Amy?"

I stare at the table. It seems the only topic of conversation is death. I rip another chunk of pizza with my teeth. It takes me longer to chew it. The pizza seems to roll around my mouth for too many seconds until all the flavour is drained out of it. I gulp it down, almost choking when grief makes it lodge in my throat for a second. After wiping my hands, I stand and get us drinks. Coke for me and a beer for Dad. He smiles when I set the bottle down in front of him.

"It can't be easy for you." Dad closes his mouth around the narrow bottle opening and gulps some of the frothy golden liquid down. "When do you see the counsellor next?"

"In a few days." I don't want to admit talking to her helped a little, although not in the way my parents would want. But she's another person I have to lie to. I sigh. It's odd the only one I can talk to is Matthew and I probably shouldn't trust him at all.

"Dad..." I catch myself, filling my mouth with more pizza.

Dad raises his eyebrows, waiting for me to continue.

"Did Charley ever mention anyone called Matthew?"

"No." His lips curl into a small smile. "But then she didn't really talk to me about boys." His smile fades and his eyebrows pinch together. "Why?"

I shake my head. "No reason." It was a long shot anyway. Matthew said he didn't know Charley.

"Kim." Dad's voice contains a note of warning. He leans forward. I squirm beneath his stare.

I force my shoulders into a rigid shrug. "It's just someone I met at Charley's funeral. He seemed nice." My stomach tingles. His smile was more than nice. But everything else about him is unsettling.

"Ah." Dad's reaction is enough to tempt me into looking up.

"What?" I try not to smile, but my lips curl upwards anyway.

He wipes his hands on a sheet of kitchen towel and reaches out to me. His hand falls short. I don't bridge the gap.

"Charley didn't always hang out with the right people."

I twist my hands together in my lap.

"And if this boy, Matthew, is someone Charley never mentioned..." He draws in a breath, puffs out his cheeks and then exhales slowly. "It probably means he's bad news." He pulls his hand away from me and covers up our lack of connection by plucking up another pizza slice.

Wisdom from Dad. The thing is he's right.

"Are you going to Amy's funeral?"

I blink at the question. "I hadn't thought about it."

But now my mind is racing with the idea. I wasn't Amy's friend, so I have no right to go. The memory of an incessant rhythm floats into my head. Matthew will be there.

"I'd like to go. For Charley."

Dad smiles. "It's a nice thought." His voice is full of pride.

My skin prickles with guilt. He pulls his wallet out of his pocket and tugs out a twenty-pound note. He holds it out to me.

"Get some flowers from us all."

I hesitate, staring at the note.

"Something wrong? Are flowers more expensive?"

"No." I pluck the note from his fingers. "No. Thanks, Dad." Appetite lost, I stand, cross to the other side of the table and give him a swift hug. "I think I'm going to head to bed. It's been a rough week."

I pull away, but he catches my arm. "You'd tell me if anything else was wrong, wouldn't you?" His pupils are wide with fear.

"There isn't, I promise." I trudge up the stairs, my lie haunting me with every step I take.

I catch a glimpse of my reflection in the bedroom window—faded and translucent, like a ghost. My hair melds with the glow of a street lamp, giving it the illusion of being blond. For a moment, I could believe I was staring at Charley's reflection rather than my own.

*

Sleep is the furthest thing from my mind as I boot up the desktop computer. Dad got it for Charley and me to do homework on when we were staying with him. The computer whirrs and beeps while I fiddle with the uncomfortable chair's height adjuster. The blue desktop background fades into existence. I open up a browser window and start tapping words into the search box. A logical explanation for everything has to exist and I'm going to find it.

Mind control. I quickly discover most thoughts on this topic are conspiracy theories. The more reputable theories cite sleep deprivation, sensory deprivation and social pressure as the most common methods. I don't need to read anymore to realise it's a dead end.

I push my hands through my hair, recalling all the odd things which have happened since Charley's death. I grimace. With the exception of my memory loss and Amy's death, everything revolves around Matthew. Maybe Dad's right. He is trouble.

Hypnosis. A trance state. My heart rate increases when I read a hypnotist can implant suggestions in a subject's mind. I prop my chin on my hand. My head was fuzzy around Matthew, but I was never in a trance. Was I?

I push him to the back of my mind and concentrate on Amy. Closing my eyes, I force myself to recall every horrifying moment of her death. A vile metallic stench stalks the edge of my senses and the memory of a monotonous rhythm thuds through my mind.

My shoulders slump. I could type one ridiculous theory after another into the search engine all night and still come up with nothing. I push my chair away from the table. The carpet stops it from going too far. I clutch the sides of the seat and use my toe to swing the chair left, then right, left, then right. Where can I find answers? I stare upwards as knots form in my stomach, the result of the realisation there is someone who can help me—my grief counsellor, Ms. Jones.

CHAPTER TWELVE

I have one outfit suitable for a funeral and it hasn't been long enough since I wore it. The dour skirt suit has been washed and pressed, but the taint of Charley's death clings to it, making my skin itch. I hover at the back of the church. It doesn't feel right to sit down. The church is too vast to ever be warm, despite the efforts of black pipe radiators. The combination of artificial lights and candles highlight the warm cream and amber hues of the ancient stonework. Weak autumn light filters in through tall stained-glass windows, metamorphosed into slender rays of green, purple, pink and blue.

It's only Friday. I didn't know funerals could be arranged so fast.

"What are you doing here?" Tia's voice slices through my mind.

I stare at her, my mouth hanging open in what has to be a stupid expression. Her girlfriends flank her on either side. I almost ask her the same question. She and Amy didn't get along. The girls she's with are her friends, not Amy's. I shut my mouth and bite my tongue.

"Well?" Tia folds her arms and tilts her hips. Her pursed lips and narrowed eyes scream hostility.

"I…" I take a deep breath and tell myself my reaction is ridiculous. "Charley would have wanted me to come."

Tia's upper lip curls into a sneer. She puffs air out of her nose in a silent snort. "I don't think Amy would have wanted you to."

My lips droop. What I should say is, "She definitely wouldn't have wanted you here." Instead, I'm left staring at Tia's back while she stalks down the aisle and takes a seat half way down. Legs shaking, I duck into the back pew and sink down, burying my face in a hymn book.

The service starts once the church has filled up. It's a massive turnout. Apart from the pew I'm in, they're all filled. I recognise several of the faces from Charley's funeral. Their shared friends are ashen, weary of death and the attached rituals.

Matthew isn't here. I keep glancing round, scanning the closed doorway, waiting and hoping, even though it's disrespectful.

The heartfelt hum of the priest's voice washes over me. This isn't some out-of-the-box ceremony. Every word is especially for Amy. The organ hums out baleful notes. I stand a beat behind the rest of the congregation and mutter my way through a hymn I don't know.

Halfway through the second verse, a breeze disturbs my hair. I twist round and lock gazes with Matthew. His eyebrows tug down closer to his eyes and then he vanishes out the door.

No you don't. The uneven singing masks my clumsy escape from the pew and the sound of my heels clicking across the stone floor. I grab the door before it slams shut and slip through it.

Matthew is striding down the path. I shut the door, tug my heels off and, holding them in one hand, sprint after him. Debris on the path chafes my feet and snags holes in my thin tights.

He wheels round, mouth pinched into a narrow line. "You shouldn't be here." His voice is calm and controlled, but my mind conjures venom into it.

I step into his personal space, staring up into his face. "You owe me answers."

His eyebrows rise. His mouth almost curls into a smile. "What makes you think that?"

I jab my fingertip against his chest. "Because you made me think I was going mad. Because you can't just tell me my sister and Amy were both murdered and then shut me out." I fidget from foot to foot. The chill from the flagstones is creeping up through my feet, into my legs.

"Put your shoes back on."

Scowling, I obey. The added height brings me a little closer to matching his. "So? Are you going to answer my questions or not?"

Matthew presses his lips together. It's obvious he's suppressing a smile by the way the corners of his mouth twitch.

"What would you do if I refuse?"

My mouth eases open. I couldn't do anything. "You owe me." My words sound lame.

He glances towards the closed church door.

I tug at a lock of my hair. "I know Charley didn't kill herself, but no one else believes me. You're the only person who thinks any different and I have no idea who you are." He opens his mouth to speak, but I wag my finger near his face to stop him. "And don't tell me you're Matthew. That means nothing." I sink into a crouch, hugging my knees. I can't prevent the tears that are creeping up on me. I'm sick and tired of crying. "And Amy, she walked into the traffic. I almost did the same. That's not right. It's not natural. Something's going on and you seem to know what."

Matthew drops into a crouch, putting himself on an even level to me. "I don't. That's the problem."

I meet his dark stare. "I need to know what you do. Everything. You can tell me to stop looking into Charley's and Amy's deaths until you're hoarse, but I won't." I clench my fists. "I'll never stop."

"And if you do find out what happened, what then?"

My brow crumples. "I don't understand."

"Will it bring them back?"

The tears I've been holding in threaten to form a tidal wave. I sniff them back. "Of course not." I dig my nails into my palms. "But if I know what happened, I'll be able to move on."

His eyes narrow into thoughtful half moons. "Are you sure?"

My clenched hands relax. "No." I blink my eyes, refusing to let him reduce me to tears.

"Are answers really worth risking your life for?"

I breathe in and out slowly for a few seconds. Each breath pushes my tears further down inside my gut. Each breath strengthens my resolve.

"Yes," I say. "If you'd ever lost anyone, you'd understand that."

The rigid frown lines on his forehead soften. "I do understand, Kim." He leans forward onto his knees, bringing his face closer to mine. "But I don't want to see you get hurt."

"It's not up to you to protect me."

His mouth flinches into a brief grimace.

"I will keep looking until I find answers." I force myself to stare into his endless eyes. "So if you really want to protect me, you'll tell me what you know."

"All right." His words knock the air out of my lungs. "But not here. And not now."

"Then where? When?"

He stands and glances at the church door again. "This evening, at six. At the statue of Queen Victoria."

I hesitate. The statue is at the edge of the town center, in a small park that's seldom used by anyone during the day, let alone at night. But there's a pub a stone's throw away in one direction and a nightclub directly across the main road in the other. I'd be within reach of help if I need it. I shake my head. I won't need help.

Wobbling on my ankles, I push with my hand and stand up. "I'll see you tonight."

He smiles. Every doubt in my mind flies away as my insides melt. I stand entranced, gazing at him while he wanders away.

*

A single loud knock on the door disturbs my thoughts. My forehead crumples into a frown. I'm not expecting anyone. Mum is out and Chris never knocks. I sit up when the knock is repeated and pad across my cream carpet. When I swing the door open, I come face to face with Gage. He's smiling. My mouth drops open. I didn't expect to see him in my house. A snigger erupts from the stairs. I glance past Gage and catch sight of the top of Chris's head. He's hiding on the stairs, grinning.

"Get lost, Chris."

He stands up and saunters up the stairs. "Sure. I'll leave you and your boyfriend alone."

If I had anything to chuck at Chris, I would, but instead I swing my hand through the air. Chris laughs and ducks into his room. Cheeks flushed, I turn back to Gage. His lips are sucked in and his cheeks are puffed out. His chest and shoulders shudder with a silent, wheezing laugh. I narrow my eyes, prompting Gage's laugh to explode out of him.

"I'm sorry." His apology would carry more weight if he wasn't still laughing so hard that his eyes are starting to water. "Can I come in?"

I've half a mind to tell him to get lost. But I don't. I step aside, allowing him into the room. He makes himself comfortable on my bed, sprawling back onto one elbow. I take up residence on my desk chair, tucking my feet beneath my bottom.

"What are you doing here?" I can't forget that Amy told me he was trouble.

Gage whistles and holds up his hand. "No need to be so frosty." He's finally gained control of his laughter, but is still grinning. The smile persists as he tries to ease his lips into a straight, sombre line. "I heard that Tia gave you a hard time at the funeral earlier. I wanted to make sure you were okay."

If he was trouble, he wouldn't care if I was okay.

I tilt my head to the side, frowning. "You weren't there?"

He shrugs. "Funerals aren't my thing, but I know most of the guys who were. They said Tia told you to leave and that you did."

I press my lips together to stop a gasp from slipping out. Of course that's what people would have thought. I make a show of twiddling my fingers together in my lap.

"I'm fine. She was probably right. I shouldn't have been at the funeral."

Gage rubs at his cleanly shaved chin. "You had as much right as anyone else."

"I wasn't Amy's friend."

"No, but Charley was." He begins to make a spiral with his fingertip on my crumpled quilt, now an embarrassing chintz design, in and then out again, in and then out again.

I shake myself and force my gaze away from his hypnotic action.

"I'm sorry," he says.

I chuckle. "I'm hearing those words a lot at the moment." I use my hips to swivel the seat to the left and then back round to the right. "You don't need to apologise for Tia. You're her boyfriend, not her keeper."

Gage sits up and angles his muscular body towards me. "I was apologising for bringing Charley up. It was insensitive of me." His voice is low with a rumbling rasp to it. I can see why Charley dated him.

I shrug and allow the chair to swing still. He stands and takes cautious steps towards me. I remain motionless, chest hurting with the inability to breathe, as he kneels down in front of me.

"Charley was a wonderful girl." He takes my hands and uses his thumbs to stroke my skin.

Something stirs and flutters in the pit of my stomach. I swallow and stare into his eyes, which are void of longing or desire. He's here as a friend, nothing more.

"It must have been horrible for you to find her."

I gaze at my hands, small in comparison to his.

"I'm sorry. We don't have to talk about this if it hurts too much."

I blink tears away. "We've nothing to talk about."

His thumbs stop tracing circles over my skin. He moves his head, making it impossible for me to avoid eye contact without physically turning away.

"I don't remember. Mum, Dad, the police… they told me I found Charley, but I don't remember." I haven't uttered those words to anyone outside of my family, Sophie and the shrink. "Apparently it's lacunar amnesia, or something." I pull my right hand away from Gage and massage my temple. "I have a gap in my memory. I'll probably never get it back."

I sigh, dropping my hand to my lap. "I don't want it back." I clear my throat to stop tears choking me. "I want to remember Charley happy and vibrant." I focus on Gage and the strong curve of his jaw and bright blue eyes. I could tell him anything. Ask him anything. "She was happy, wasn't she?"

He nods. "She always seemed to be." His shoulders hunch up to his ears and sag down again in a slow, dramatic shrug. "You knew her better than me, or any of her friends. What do you think?"

"I think she was murdered." I blurt the words out too quickly to take them back.

Gage's eyes widen. I search his face, trace the taut muscles in his cheeks, the sharp upwards angle of his eyebrows, the way his lips part enough to reveal teeth that are too white and too perfect to be natural. His Adam's apple bobs up and down several times.

"What makes you think that?"

"She was happy, laughing… She was normal. Nothing was amiss. Except…"

"Except?"

I shrug. "She got a text and went home ahead of me. I was twenty minutes behind her, tops." My harsh breathing makes my chest and shoulders heave. "To kill yourself, there has to be some terrible reason, doesn't there? But Charley was popular. She was going places. It doesn't make sense."

Gage straightens his thighs and wraps his arms around my back. His embrace is strong and comforting. I sink against his chest, burying my face against his broad shoulder.

"I thought you said you didn't remember." His deep, rumbling voice vibrates against me, soothing me.

I squeeze my eyes shut. "I don't. I remember walking home and then I woke up in hospital."

"Maybe there's something none of us knew."

I clench his maroon jumper in my fists. "She told me everything."

"Everything?" Gage says, amusement in his voice.

I breathe in sharply. Heat flushes my cheeks. "Maybe not everything."

He pushes me away from him and holds my shoulders, preventing me from flopping forward again. "Maybe it wasn't just her sex life that she kept secret. Do you know who the text message was from?"

I shake my head too quickly, making the room spin. "She deleted it."

Gage raises one hand to my face, cupping my jaw in his hand while he uses his thumb to wipe the tears from my cheeks.

"I know it's hard, but I think you do have to accept that Charley committed suicide."

"I can't." I push his hand away. "I won't." I slide out from his grip and the chair, covering the distance to the door in four long strides. "I think you should go."

Gage uses the chair to help him stand and crosses over to me. He holds my shoulders again. "Kim…"

I sweep his hands away. "You came here to apologise. You've done that. Now go." I open the door and point down the stairs. "And don't worry, I won't tell Tia you were here."

He steps back as though my words carry a venomous sting. I push down the guilt that shivers through me.

Gage brushes his mocha hair behind his ear. "You're not going to be able to move on until you accept what Charley did. I'll see myself out." He brushes past me and takes the steps two at a time.

I shut my door and lean against it. The barrier doesn't block out the slam of the front door.

*

Ms. Jones's office is like a time warp. Nothing has changed since the last time I was here, except she's wearing a different outfit—a plum coloured skirt suit with a cream blouse. She smiles when I sit down. My gaze drifts to the file on her lap. My file.

This is the first day she could fit me in, but now I'm here, my stomach feels like it's stuffed with golf balls. Acid burns my chest.

I take a deep breath and clench my fists in my lap. "I want to remember."

Ms. Jones's expression remains neutral.

"I want you to hypnotise me."

Her eyebrows rise. "Kim…"

I shuffle forward so I'm sitting on the very edge of the seat. "Please. I need to remember."

"Why?"

I jerk my head back. I'm not sure how to answer her question. The only thing I know for sure is I can't tell her the truth. I want to get my memories back in the hope I'll remember a clue, something to help me discover why Charley died, something to tell Matthew.

"I fitted you in because you sounded frantic on the phone," Ms. Jones says. "Has something happened?"

"No. Nothing's happened." Except the impossible. The way Amy died. Matthew talking into my mind.

Ms. Jones picks up my file and leafs through it. "I need you to be honest with me, Kim. Has something happened?"

"You mean aside from my sister dying and me not being able to remember a damn thing about it?" I stand up and pace the length of the room.

I'm not going to apologise for snapping. I put my hands on my stomach and take several deep breaths.

"My life feels like it's spinning out of control. I thought I knew Charley." I thought I knew what was and wasn't possible. "A friend told me I have to move on. How can I do that with this big gap in my memory?" I fold my arms, waiting for Ms. Jones to refuse.

She closes my file. "Hypnosis might not work. We don't

fully understand what causes amnesia."

My eyes widen. "But you'll try?"

"With your parents' permission."

"But I'm sixteen."

"And you still live with your parents. They must consent to any treatment you receive."

I should have known. I stalk over to my coat, pull my phone out and select Dad's number. "Call Dad. Now. He'll say yes." I hope. Mum certainly won't.

When Ms. Jones doesn't take the phone from me, I hit the call button and press it to my ears. The ring tone repeats three too many times before Dad finally picks up.

"Kim?" His voice is slightly crackly over the phone. "Are you okay?"

No. "I'm at Ms. Jones's office." My mouth becomes dry as I wait for Dad to say something. "I want her to hypnotise me to remember what happened the night Charley died." I sniffle down the phone for good measure. "But she needs your permission."

I glance at Ms. Jones. She's sitting absolutely still, watching me.

"Dad?" I wish I could see his expression, so I could guess what he was thinking.

"Let me speak to Ms. Jones."

Scowling, I hand the phone to her.

She accepts it. "Wait outside, please, Kim."

I huff as I storm out of the room, too angry to care that I'm acting like a brat. The receptionist glances at me, before busying herself with typing. Her fingers clack quickly across the keyboard, filling the silence. No one else is in the waiting room. I sit down, but almost instantly stand again. How long does it take to say 'yes' or 'no'?

I spin round when the office door opens. Ms. Jones beckons me back inside and hands me my phone as I stride past her.

"Well? What did Dad say?"

Ms. Jones motions for me to sit down. I ignore her.

"Your father is worried about you."

I press my hands against my thighs. "But did he agree to the hypnosis?"

"He's not very happy about it…"

"Great. Just great."

"But… if it's what you really want, then he's willing to agree to it."

I freeze, shocked. "He said yes?"

Ms. Jones nods.

I slip into the spare seat, fingertips tingling with anticipation. "Let's do it."

She glances up at the wall clock. My heart sinks. She probably has another appointment. She did fit me in after all.

"I don't usually work past five," she says in a matter of fact tone. She wants to go home.

I suck my lower lip in to stop it quivering and prevent myself from begging her to stay.

"But I'll make an exception."

The clock's minute hand clunks round. I'm meant to be meeting Matthew in less than an hour.

"How long will this take?" I shouldn't be worrying about the time, when she's offering to stay late.

"You can make an appointment for another day," she says, noticing my glance at the clock.

Another day? I need answers now. "No. Now is fine." Matthew will wait for me. He has to.

"All right. Remember I told you it might not work, Kim. You have to prepare yourself for the fact hypnosis might not achieve anything." She smiles kindly. "Why don't you make yourself comfortable?"

I'm torn between excitement and fear as I sit back in the chair. The back is too high and straight to be comfortable, but I do my best to relax. Shadows start to gather in the room as the sun drifts down towards the horizon.

"I'd like you to relax and concentrate on your breathing. Take nice deep breaths. In and out. In and out." Her tone is low and soothing. "Close your eyes."

I obey, eager to remember. Echoes of light punctuate the darkness behind my closed eyelids. My chest rises and falls with deep controlled breaths, but my body is tense and my mind is alert.

"Imagine you're walking down a flight of steps. I want you to count each one out loud."

"One… two." My voice rattles around my consciousness. "Three… four… five." The drone of traffic on the street outside Ms. Jones's office fades to nothingness. "Six… seven… eight… nine." All my muscles relax and my body melts into the chair. "Ten… eleven." My voice begins to slur. "Twelve." I allow my heavy head to flop back against the chair. "Thirteen… fourteen." I'm weightless. Floating. Yet at the same time my limbs feel heavy. I can't move my fingers. I should be alarmed, but I'm too relaxed to care.

Ms. Jones's quiet voice breaks into the dark recesses of my mind. "I want you to imagine you're in a room, somewhere you feel safe."

I'm sitting on my old bed, in my old room, in my old house, the one we lived in before Mum and Dad split up. I know where I am, but the details are hazy, like I'm sitting in a fog bank. But I feel safe and warm. I curl up on the bed and inhale the floral scent of the fabric softener Mum uses.

"The door to this room will always be open." A door manifests in response to Ms. Jones's instructions. "If you need to, come back to this room." The door swings open, revealing a dark corridor. "If you're happy to continue, raise your left forefinger."

My forefinger twitches up as though pulled by a string.

"I want you to go back to the last time you saw Charley. Why did you split up?"

"She got a text and went ahead."

The memory is vivid, as though it's happening all over again. I can see the crease lines at the top of Charley's nose forming and getting deeper as she reads the text. I can see her forced smile as she tucks her phone away and flicks her hair over her shoulder, in the way she always did when she was pretending everything was okay. *"Mind if I head home? You'll be okay getting food, won't you?"*

"I stayed behind to get takeout."

"Good. You get the takeout and then you're walking home."

I move like I'm on autopilot, getting off the bed and trudging towards the door, into the darkness. It feels like I'm really moving, but I'm sitting still, paralysed in the armchair. I'm in the street, hurrying through the biting cold. Darkness gathers around me. My heartbeat quickens as I jump at shadows all over again. The white carrier bag is heavy in my hand. The scent of rich sauces rises from the bag and hangs around me, making my stomach rumble.

"You arrive home."

I'm standing in front of my red door, frozen.

"What do you do?"

Nothing. I can't think. I can't move. I'm at the door, but the edges of my memory are frayed and the scene is blanched of every sense except sight.

"Do you go inside?"

I must have done. How would I get inside? My keys. I reach into my pocket, but it's like a black hole with only endless space inside. No phone, no keys, nothing. I glance away from the solid doors to the windows, but they're opaque, preventing me from looking inside.

My breathing quickens.

"Try to relax, Kim. Remember, you can go back to your safe place if you need to."

I don't want to. I want to get inside. I have to get to Charley. Panic sets in. I fumble for keys, which aren't there, shoving my hand deeper and deeper into the vast emptiness of my coat pocket.

"Do you open the door?"

I push the door with my fingertips. It swings open. Didn't Charley lock it behind her? Inky blackness pours into my memory, accompanied by a scent so familiar, I could almost believe I've conjured it myself. Freshly cut grass. Blood throbs round my body so fast my arteries ache and threaten to burst. My heart is ready to pop out of my chest as a single word slips into my head—*"forget"*—spoken by an achingly familiar voice. Matthew.

CHAPTER THIRTEEN

I don't know what to think, feel or believe. I stumble away from Ms. Jones's office, towards the edge of the city center and the small park where I agreed to meet Matthew. I must be stupid, or mad. He made me forget. Was he there when I discovered Charley? My mind is foggy. My memories of the evening she died are still lost.

I stop when I realise where I am—the police station. It seems like weeks ago when I last stood outside instead of days. I could go in and tell them Matthew is responsible for my amnesia. They wouldn't listen. Every word that would tumble out of my mouth would sound like the ravings of an insane person. They wouldn't search for Matthew. They'd lock me up. Minds can't be controlled with a single word. Telepathy doesn't exist. But what other explanation is there?

Only one person can give me answers.

It's already dark. The loop road, which lies between me and the park, is packed full of stationary cars. Engines rumble and acrid fumes hang in mini-clouds in the chilly air. The skeletal trees in the park have been adorned with strings of pale blue lights. It looks pretty. Welcoming.

I break into a run, weaving between cars as I dash across the road and into the empty park. The walls and trees muffle the sound of the traffic.

"Matthew." I shout his name into the darkness.

I glance around. The paths wrap round the statue of Queen

Victoria and two empty flowerbeds edged with rocks. The queen stands tall and plump on a column, her double chins proudly thrust into the sky.

"Matthew?" I should leave, not stand here willing him to come.

I squeeze my eyes shut and count as I inhale and exhale, forcing each breath to enter or leave my body to a calming count of five. If he was dangerous, wouldn't I be dead by now? Or maybe this is part of his treacherous game. I swing down and grab a fist-sized rock. I have no idea if I'd actually have the guts to use it, but somehow its lumpy presence steadies my nerves.

"Kim."

My heart booms against my ribcage. I swing round, tightening my grip on the rock. Matthew is standing a short distance away, bathed in the gentle blue glow of the tree-lights. His eyes narrow slightly when he notices the rock in my hand.

I suck in a breath. "I want answers. Now."

"What's the rock for?"

I raise it to my chest. "Protection. From you."

His face becomes blank.

"I wanted to remember what happened the night Charley died. I wanted to fill the void in my mind." I gesture wildly towards my head. "It didn't work. But do you know what I did remember?"

He shakes his head slowly.

"Your voice telling me to forget." I almost scream when he remains silent.

He continues to watch me, expression utterly unreadable.

"What are you?" I spit the words out and punctuate them with three paces forward, almost closing the distance between us. "What did you do to me?"

He folds his arms. "Put the rock down and we can talk."

His calm voice ignites my anger. "You can control my mind," I screech, tugging in sharp breaths so I can yell again. "You made me forget. Why?" My eyes grow wide. Tears cloud my vision. "You were there, weren't you? At my house the night Charley died."

"I did make you forget." His admission stabs at my heart and steals my breath. "I stopped you from walking into a road, too." His impenetrably dark eyes will me to believe in him. The weird thing is I do. Instantly.

My hand relaxes, releasing the rock, which thuds to the ground and fractures, revealing soft white chalk.

"You can control minds?"

"When I have to, yes."

"Impossible." My voice lacks any conviction, as my sense of what's possible spins around me, taunting me.

Matthew takes a few hesitant steps towards me, his gaze piercing mine and holding me tighter the closer he gets.

I edge back, shaking my head. "It's impossible," I say again.

"What do you want me to say?" Sadness clings to his features, making his mouth droop.

I stand my ground, determined to drag answers out of him this time. "Why did you steal my memories?"

"I didn't steal them. I shut them away." He rubs the side of his neck. "I'd like to say it was to protect you from what you'd seen, but I'd be lying." His voice is so mournful my anger begins to evaporate from my consciousness. "I was protecting myself."

"From what?" Only one answer makes any sense. "Did you kill Charley?"

He shakes his head. "No." Honesty rings in the velvet depths of his voice, so powerful and earnest I can feel it.

I wipe the tears away from my eyes. "Then who did? You know what happened to her, don't you?"

He bows his head. "You need to let this go, Kim."

"I can't. You promised me answers."

He starts to shake his head again.

I slap him hard across the face. "You promised." I clap my hands to my mouth, more shocked at lashing out than he appears to be.

He stalks away, shoulders hunched.

"Liar." My accusation pulls him to a halt.

Slowly, he turns round. His teeth are clenched, his face taut. "What?"

"You're a liar, Matthew."

Tension makes his body rigid.

I begin to count things off on my fingers. "You say you made me forget what happened so I wouldn't remember you. Well, that's bull, isn't it? You showed up at Charley's funeral, bold as brass. Then outside the nightclub you picked me up and saw me safely home. You were at the school. Do I have to go on?"

While I've been talking, Matthew's eyes have narrowed.

"And what was that the other day in the park? *Clarity*? You used your…" I wave my hand, trying to think of a label that doesn't sound too insane, "magic… to let me think clearly around you." I fold my arms and close the distance between us. "You can try to convince yourself that you're protecting yourself, but you're not. You're protecting me." I jab him in the chest. "You admitted it earlier today, when you said you didn't want me to get hurt."

Matthew's eyebrows hood his eyes, but he remains silent.

"But guess what? I don't need your help. I don't need you to order me around, or steal my memories. I don't need you to lie to me." I press my finger against him, pushing with all my might, but he doesn't flinch or back away. "All I need is to find out what happened to my sister. So no, I won't let it go. And I want you to keep out of my way."

He swats my hand away. His dark stare is so intense I start to quiver, but I don't back down.

"Or better still, let me remember what I saw the night Charley died."

"No."

"You locked my memories away. Undo what you did." I plant my hands on my hips and stare up at him, daring him to defy me. "Well?"

For a second it looks like he might say something.

"Is everything all right?"

I swing round to face the owner of the voice. A policeman is standing at the edge of the park, one hand on his radio, the other on the baton looped through his belt. He strides towards me.

I start to nod, glancing over my shoulder at Matthew at the same time. I freeze. He's gone.

"Who were you talking to?" I jump at the close proximity of the officer's voice. "You seem upset."

I swallow away the anger bubbling up within me, shrug, smile and shake my head. "I'm rehearsing for a play." It's probably the lamest thing I could have said, aside from, "I was talking to a guy who's just disappeared. Again."

The officer's eyebrows slither up his forehead. "Excuse me?"

I force my lips into an even wider smile. "I'm rehearsing for a play. Shakespeare. Hamlet. I'm playing Ophelia." My choice of character isn't totally random. Ophelia went mad because of a man.

The officer purses his lips. "Well, next time less shouting in public places, all right?" He glances around the park, shrugs and wanders off.

I turn round in a slow circle, peering into all the dark recesses of the park. I ball my hands into fists. Matthew has vanished. I clench my teeth. Coward.

CHAPTER FOURTEEN

"Someone made me forget what I saw," I say quietly.

Kevin sucks in a sharp breath. "I don't understand."

After a sleepless night and stumbling through the morning like a zombie, I needed to speak to someone. I didn't know who else to turn to. The record store is quiet, allowing me a few minutes to unload on Kevin just outside.

I tap the side of my head. "I'm missing memories from the night Charley died. It isn't natural. Someone made me forget. Why would they do that if it wasn't murder?"

It's a good question. I'm already convinced Matthew lied about his motives. Never mind my real theory is at odds with the words that just gushed from my mouth. I long for Kevin to say something, but he just stands still, gawking at me.

"My grief counsellor hypnotised me yesterday, to see if I could remember what I saw when I found Charley."

"But you couldn't?" Kevin asks.

"No. But I did remember someone telling me to forget."

Kevin's face has drained of colour. My heart lurches. Maybe now he's finally starting to believe me, instead of dismissing my ramblings as mad or irrational.

"Someone?" His eyebrows rise in time with his voice. "Who?"

I click my tongue against my teeth, not knowing how much to say. "I remember the instruction, not who gave it." My words are careful. It isn't a complete lie. I have no visual memory of

Matthew ordering me to forget. I hope Kevin didn't notice my hesitation.

"Instruction?"

"A single word. Forget. It was a male voice," I add, hoping it will make my words ring true.

Kevin paces back and forth. He doesn't seem to notice the scowls of the shoppers who swerve to avoid him. He stops, standing closer to me than before. His minty breath is warm on my cool face. "You realise it isn't possible?" His voice is trembling, despite the sense in his words.

I glare at him. Before all this madness started, I would have agreed with him. But now I know it *is* possible, even if I don't know *how*.

"Have you told anyone else?"

I narrow my eyes. Was I wrong to trust him? "No."

His shoulders relax a little. He takes hold of my hands. "Kim, we haven't known each other long but…"

"No, we haven't." My voice is sharp as I cut him off.

His head bobs a couple of times. "But I care about you. I'm worried about what might happen if you go around telling people about what you think you remember."

I wrench my hands away from his grip. He doesn't believe me. "You think I'll get carted off to the looney bin?"

He stares at me open mouthed for a couple of seconds. "Yes. Something like that." He grins stiffly. "You have to admit, it does sound pretty crazy."

I throw my hands up and turn my back on him.

"I don't think you are crazy." Kevin hurries round, cutting in front of me. "I know you believe someone made you forget…"

I raise my chin. "Someone did." Matthew *did*.

"But maybe it's your grief fabricating events, so you don't have to face what Charley did." He reaches out to me, but I flinch away. "What did your counsellor say when you told…?"

"Her," I finish for him. I open and close my mouth.

"You didn't tell her," Kevin sighs as he guesses the truth behind my fish impression.

I shake my head and gaze at the ground. I can't explain why I didn't. This time, I don't pull away when Kevin rubs my arm.

"If you really believed it, you would have told her."

I can't argue with him. Not without telling Kevin everything and sounding even more insane than he already thinks I am. Defeated, my shoulders slump.

Kevin's hand slides down my arm and catches hold of my hand. "I have to go back into work. Can I call you later? Maybe we can talk about all this some more."

I nod, making no effort to look up or say goodbye as he hesitantly heads back into the store.

*

Gage is sitting on my doorstep when I get home, squinting at the screen of his smart phone as my feet crunch across the gravel drive.

He tugs his earbuds out and drops them, allowing them to dangle on thin black cables. Tinny music trickles out, too quiet to be distinct.

He grins at me and jerks his thumb in the direction of my front door. "No one's home."

I tilt my head, waiting for a better explanation.

He tucks his phone into his jeans pocket and stands. "I couldn't stop thinking about yesterday and how much I must have pissed you off." He closes the distance between us. "I want to make things right." He flicks a curl of hair from my shoulder. "Can I come in?"

I should refuse. I knock his hand away from where it's lingered on my shoulder. Now he's closer, the music piping through his earbuds is clear enough to hear. It's a heavy rock tune. My nose wrinkles as I catch a whiff of rusted metal. My gut lurches, telling me I should recognise the scent, but my mind crashes with confusion.

"I think you should go," I say. I don't need to be told to get over Charley's death again.

Gage's expression becomes sombre. He steps into my personal space—so close our bodies are almost touching. My cheeks flush with warmth. Imagining my neighbours twitching their curtains, I back away, twist round Gage and jam my key into the lock.

"You should go." My voice is firmer.

His hand closes over mine as I fumble to turn the key. He twists and the lock clunks, as he presses his chest against my back.

"What do you want, Gage?" It's hard to talk when my breath doesn't want to leave my throat.

"To talk."

I push the door open, step inside, wheel round and press my palms against his chest before he has a chance to close the gap again. "You've got a funny way of showing it."

"Okay," he admits. "Maybe I want to do more than talk." He runs his fingers over my hand as it rests on the door. "Haven't you figured it out yet, Kim?"

Amy was right. Gage is trouble. I don't dare assume this is real. A hot guy, two years older, wouldn't be remotely interested in me. A guy with a girlfriend. Did he and Charley break up because he couldn't keep his hands off other girls?

"Do you know why I dumped Charley?"

I shrug, pretending not to be phased that he guessed what I was thinking. "She broke up with you."

Gage shakes his head, a slow smile creeping across his lips. "Is that what she told you?"

"Yes," I say, even though it's a lie. Charley didn't talk about their break up at all. Tension makes my body stiff.

"I broke up with her because I realised it was you I wanted."

I snort a laugh, hardly the most attractive thing I've ever done. "You don't know me, Gage."

"I saw you with Charley. Watched how you wilted in her shadow. Saw how beautiful you were." His hand moves from mine, to cup my jaw. He tilts my head upwards, forcing me to look directly into his warm eyes. "But I never had the guts to tell you." The husky sound of his voice and the background hum of the bass guitar through his earbuds are enough to hook me.

"You're with Tia." My quivering voice doesn't hold the conviction of my words.

"I wouldn't be if you didn't want me to be." He doesn't give me time to consider the ramifications of his words. Instead he reels me in, leans down and presses his lips against mine. The moist warmth of his kiss flows into my lips and floods my body with warmth.

He breaks off, but stays close enough so his lips brush against mine as he speaks. "Can I come in?" His breath drifts over my face and I inhale his musky, metallic tinged scent.

I've never wanted to say "yes" more in my life.

"I don't think it's a good idea," I whisper.

Something in my mind screams none of this is true. How could it be?

And then he kisses me again. In the same instant he wraps his free arm around the small of my back, teasing my coat and T-shirt up a little. Energy pulses up my spine as his fingertips tickle my skin.

"Can I come in?" This time he whispers the question into my ear, stroking my chin and back.

My voice is paralysed, so I simply nod and allow him to guide me into the house. He hooks the door with his foot, kicking it shut with a thud.

Propelling me towards the stairs, Gage closes his mouth over mine again. My entire body melts into his embrace.

"Shall we go to your room?"

His question feels more like a command to my trembling body. I stiffen.

He nuzzles my jaw with his lips and nose. "What's wrong?"

A command. Matthew used words to command me. I tug away, throwing myself off balance, and fall from Gage's embrace. I land hard on the stairs, jarring my spine.

"Are you all right?" Gage's expression is a mask of concern. He holds his hand out to me. "Did I do something wrong?"

I shake my head slowly. Gage is not Matthew.

Continuing to hold his hand out, he takes a half step back.

"I'm sorry. I didn't mean to freak you out. Can we just go upstairs and talk?"

That word again. I've lost count of the number of times he's suggested we "talk". I push myself up one step, widening the gap between us.

"I don't think it's a good idea," I whisper.

My head might not, but my body does. My attention has drifted from his face to the definition of his strong muscles beneath his fitted T-shirt. Why isn't he wearing a coat and a jumper?

"Really?" The corners of his mouth push up into a cheeky grin. "You've been through hell recently, Kim. Why not give in and have a little fun?"

Why not? Because my life is insane right now. Because I'm grieving for my sister, his ex-girlfriend. Because Mum could come home at any second. A million more reasons why I should throw Gage out of the house fill my head, but I can't vocalise any of them.

He moves forward again, bracing his body with his arm as he leans in to kiss me. I pull away until my back is resting against the edge of the stairs. I have nowhere else to go and, as his lips connect with mine, I realise I don't want to run away at all.

The track on his mp3 player has changed to a sultry jazz tune, with a strong, sexy, saxophone solo. I push my mouth against his with a desperate urgency. He tugs the zipper of my coat down, peels the thick garment from my shoulders and tosses it into the hallway. My sense drops away with my coat and I find myself clasping my hands at the back of his thick neck.

Gage pulls away, grabs my hand and tugs me up the stairs. We take them two at a time, barrel into my room and collapse onto my bed, arms wrapped around one another's backs, mouths inseparable. His tongue teases at my lips, gently prising them apart to slip inside my mouth. I've always dreaded this moment, assuming I'd want to gag, but it feels absolutely natural and before long, my tongue is dancing with his.

My body aches when Gage pulls away. He retrieves his phone from his pocket, peering around my room. He grins when he sees my speaker dock and saunters over to it.

"I thought we could listen to some music while we talk."

I don't want to talk and from his behaviour, nor does he.

He slots his phone into the dock and quickly selects some music. The sensual jazz tune floods through the speakers, floating over me, intensifying my desire. The metallic stench becomes richer, filling the air and flooding my body. And then I recognise it. Still, I can't bring myself to care that the last time I smelt it was when Amy died. All I want is Gage.

I arch my spine in answer to him as he sits beside me on the bed, allowing him to firmly place his hand on the small of my back. He rests his chest against mine. His warm kisses make my mind swim and my last remaining rational thoughts are drowned in the seductive rhythm of the music.

His fingertips tuck my hair behind my ear. "I want you to feel like you can tell me anything."

The only sound I make is a soft murmur, as I lift my head to push my lips against his again. I clench his short hair in my fingers. My lips caress his in time to the music. Each time the cry of the saxophone rises into a yearning keen, my body is pulled to his.

"The night Charley died…" His fingers trail behind my ear, curving down to rest across my neck. "Do you remember anything at all?"

His question is inappropriate, but my mind is too lost to care. I sweep up to kiss him again, but he pushes himself up so he's a breath away from me. I groan and allow my head to sag back.

Gage strokes my bared neck. "Anything?" His question is timed with the mournful call of a trombone. The two sounds intertwine into a deep rumbling bass line that teases an answer out of my mouth.

"I was told to forget what happened."

I'm rewarded with a long, slow kiss, leaving my entire body trembling with desire.

He moves his lips close to my ear. "Told?" His whisper joins with the repeated call of a trumpet, summoning the answer to the front of my mind.

"Some guy. Matthew." His name pops out of my mouth before I can stop it. Why should I care? Matthew is an infuriating liar.

Gage's fingers slide away from my neck, replaced by his lips. He leaves a trail of kisses across my skin, travelling across my throat, down towards my collarbone and the low edge of my T-Shirt.

"Who's Matthew?"

He slides his hands beneath my top and runs them across my belly, up towards my breasts. He pauses. My body cries out for more. The chords of the bass vibrate across my skin in the wake of his touch.

"Who's Matthew?"

"I don't know."

Gage growls with disappointment, making me quiver with fear. "Who's Matthew?"

His fingers start to slide away from my skin. I clamp my hands over his. The cotton of my T-Shirt separates us, but I push his hands onto my belly and lift up in an attempt to kiss him.

He arches his neck, raising his head away from my desperate lips. "Who is Matthew?"

Tears sting my eyes. How can he be so cruel? How can he drive me to the brink of yearning and then go cold?

"I don't know." I squeeze my eyes shut. It's the truth.

"Tell me."

I whimper when his fingertips play across my skin. I want to give him an answer that will make him happy.

His lips connect with mine again. His warm tongue caresses mine. The sexy tone of a baritone saxophone picks up the melody. I groan as his right hand slithers up my side.

"Tell me." He shifts to sit astride me, his weight pining me to the bed. "Tell me everything you know about him."

He bows his head to my jaw, kissing me slowly, tracing circles on my skin with his tongue.

"He was at Charley's funeral."

Gage's mouth moves a half centimetre to the right, tantalisingly closer to my lips. He kisses me again.

"And the school. But he can… stop people noticing him."

A third kiss. This time just at the corner of my mouth. His left hand mirrors the action of his right, his fingernails lightly scratching my flesh.

"He can control minds."

"Good girl." Our lips join again. His hands glide down my torso. "Losing Charley like that, you must be so miserable."

I am. A small part of my mind whimpers at me to slap him, kick him and run. But my body doesn't want to. My body wants to surrender to him and the rest of my mind longs to obey and agree with him. I hang on the next words that pour out of his mouth, waiting for his kiss to follow.

"Every day must be torture. Having to get up and remember she hated you so much, she killed herself to get away from you."

It is.

His hands work their way up the outside of my T-Shirt to embrace my neck. I meld into his kiss, press my hands against his hips and pull him closer to me. His thumbs press against my windpipe. It's an effort to breathe, but I barely try.

"You should follow her."

Despite his constraining grip, I nod.

He kisses my forehead. "I can help you, if you want."

"Yes." I can only croak the word.

He pulls away, leaving me breathless on the bed. I watch him, unable to move. My thoughts are clouded, focused only on death. He yanks my computer's power cable free and tugs my chair beneath the ceiling lamp. I close my eyes, sink into my pillow and allow the jazz rhythm to infiltrate every fibre of my being. The tune is sombre now.

Unexpectedly, it becomes the thud, thud, thud of a dance rhythm, eclipsing the horns and strings. A bitter, metallic scent floods the room. I open my heavy eyelids. My breath freezes at the sight of the makeshift noose hanging from the light, waiting for me. Gage is beside the bed, holding his hand out to me. Smiling.

My mind wars against my body, begging me to run, as my hand lifts and clasps Gage's. I know. This is how Charley died. Gage murdered her. He made her slit her wrists. He made Amy walk into the road. He'll make me slip my neck into the noose. I'm powerless to resist him.

He pulls me from the bed into a warm embrace. I shudder. He tilts my chin upwards. His touch is so soft, so sensual. He kisses me and my body responds with false desire.

"This is what you want," he says, leading me towards the chair.

My head nods. "Yes." My voice doesn't feel like my own.

We reach the chair and he kisses me again. My eyes flutter shut. I'm going to die.

My fingers twitch into loosely clenched fists, the only action that truly feels like mine. It can't end like this. My brain orders my arm to strike Gage, but I don't move except when he half-coaxes and half-lifts me onto the chair. Tears trickle down my face, clouding my vision. The constant thud of the music hammers in time with my heart.

Gage is still smiling, his face serene as he nods to the noose. "Go on."

My hands lift at his command. I won't let this happen. Matthew.

Gage wraps his hand around my waist and presses his cheek against my stomach. "Go on." His deep voice urges my hands into action.

Matthew saved me from walking into the traffic. His commands are stronger than Gage's. My fingertips curl around the black cord. In my mind, I scream Matthew's name over and over in a discordant rhythm to the beat of the music.

Brilliant light coalesces outside my window. Gage's body tenses. Still embracing me, he twists his head. Anger ripples through his body and he clutches me harder. Grinding his teeth together, he stares up at me, his face contorting in rage.

"Do it. Now."

"Don't." Matthew's voice is in my mind. "Relax."

Relief washes through me. My body becomes liquid and I slip through Gage's arms to the floor.

"Run."

Gage tries to grab me, but I kick and scramble away towards the window. His body slams into my legs, pinning me to the ground. I scream, twist, kick, slap. Gage pulls himself up my body and clamps his hands around my throat again, squeezing. My arms flail wildly until my fingers close around my alarm clock. I grab it and smash it against Gage's head. Yelling, he pulls back and releases me.

I propel myself backwards until I slam into the wall beneath the window. Gage comes at me again, snarling, fingers tensed into a claw-like visage. I turn my back on him and struggle with the window lock. His hand clasps the back of my head. He wrenches my neck back and slams my face against the glass.

Dazed, I almost sag to the ground. His hands wrap around my neck once more. He squeezes harder this time, crushing my windpipe. I can't breathe. Bile pushes up from my stomach into my throat where it becomes trapped, burning me. My vision fades in and out. My fingers tingle, but I manage to flip the lock open and force the window up.

Blinding light floods into the room. Shrieking, Gage throws his arms up to cover his face as he falls away from me, collapsing to the floor. I clamp my eyelids shut, but the intensity of the light floods through, burning my retinas. My voice erupts out of me in a high-pitched scream.

The light is sucked away, leaving red blotchy imprints on my eyelids. I force them open and cringe against the wall, heart thundering in my chest, limbs rendered immobile in terror and awe.

Matthew is here.

CHAPTER FIFTEEN

Except Matthew isn't the same. A brilliant white clings to his outline, while dark shadows hang on his naked torso and face, magnifying the dark wells of his eyes. Light sprouts from his shoulder blades, arcing up and back to form a fountain of mottled white feathers. His jaw is rigid and his shoulders are tense.

He is the most beautiful and terrifying creature I've ever seen.

He gestures towards the door. "Get out of here, Kim." It's an instruction, not an order.

I glance at the door, but to reach it I'd have to scurry past them both. I don't think I can stand. Every nerve in my body is ablaze with fear and exhaustion. I almost died. Matthew is an angel?

Gage raises his hand, palm held upwards. The music answers his call. The dance rhythm thunders through my body, jangling my nerves and reigniting my desire to die. Like a puppet, I lurch to my feet. I try to fight Gage's pull, but my legs propel me towards him.

Matthew moves to intercept, his body as fluid as a shadow. But Gage is faster, snaking his hand out to coil it around my ankle. I want to fight, but all I can do is scream as he hauls himself up my body. His powerful arm wraps around my neck, squeezing. I hang like a rag doll in his arms, as he drapes my body in front of his. Pain stabs my chest, as though every vessel in my heart has just burst.

For a second, Matthew falters and then he darts towards my desk. He wrenches Gage's phone from the speaker dock and crumples it in his hand. The music stops abruptly, but the ghost of the beat continues to pulse through my veins.

"Are you all they've sent?" Gage says. "I'm insulted. I'm worthy of more than one of the Changed."

My brow crumples. It sounds like Matthew should be the one who's insulted, but his grim expression doesn't shift at all.

"The question is, Shamari, what's more important to you? Taking me back or saving this human's life?"

My darkening mind latches onto two words. Shamari. Human. Matthew's eyes meet mine. They droop miserably and, if I wasn't already passing out, I'd crumble under their intensity.

"I won't let you hurt her," he says, almost snarling.

Gage chuckles. "Too late." He runs his fingers down the side of my face.

I shudder at the memory of welcoming his touch. Every part of my body feels dirty, polluted. It was the music. It contained strange magic that seized control of my mind and body. Gage tilts my head to the side and kisses my cheek. I whimper and try to pull away, but his grip on my neck is too tight.

Matthew edges forwards, but Gage tuts and squeezes a little tighter.

Rage boils in the pit of my stomach. I fling my arms up, digging my nails into Gage's flesh. He snarls into my ear and flexes his arm muscles. My throat constricts under the pressure of his strength.

"Can't you kill an angel without hiding behind me?" I ask. My head throbs with the rush of blood.

Gage's grip on my neck relaxes. He starts to laugh, his chest heaving with the exertion. "She thinks you're an angel."

Then he begins to sing. His voice oozes like suffocating algae, strangling the air. An overwhelming despair grips me, trapping me in a quagmire of hopelessness. The metallic stench of Gage's magic makes me want to vomit.

Black tendrils slither over Matthew's head, curling into his eyes, nose and mouth. The oily magic reaches over his shoulders, as he tries to stride forward, fist raised. Gage's voice rises in volume and pitch and, in answer to his command, the black coils pin Matthew's arms to his chest. They wrap around his legs, smothering him in a grisly cocoon.

His gaze flicks to mine for a second. It's a second that might as well be an eternity. I stare back, silently willing him—begging him—not to give up. He raises his head, clenches his teeth and staggers sluggishly forward. But Gage's magic clutches him. He falls back and slams against the wall, sliding to the floor. A spider's web of cracks is left in the plaster.

Gage tosses me aside. I land on the floor with a grunt, pain shooting through my wrists as they break my fall. I stare at Matthew, watching as his fingertip quickly traces two shallow arcs on my carpet, one the inverse of the other. They glow dully for a second and then his voice whispers into my mind.

"Clarity."

In the same instant, my mind snaps free of Gage's control. Fighting tears, I dig my nails into the carpet and drag myself along the floor. I reach the chair and use it to pull myself to my feet. Legs shaking, I grip the seat.

I will not let him hurt Matthew any more. I dig deep to summon the strength I need. I picture Charley in my mind, alive and happy, before Gage wrenched her from me. I picture Matthew's brilliant smile and the way it makes me melt and feel utterly and completely safe. Screaming, I lift the chair and dart forward, slamming it against Gage's head.

For a second, he doesn't react at all. Then he keels over and crashes to the floor.

Sobbing, I allow the chair to drop from my hands. I crumple to my knees and stare at the blood oozing from Gage's head.

With a cry, Matthew rips himself free of the black tendrils, though impenetrable darkness still encases his body. Every movement sends spasms of pain through his tortured face, as he rises to his knees and grabs Gage by the collar, pulling him up. He presses his thumb against Gage's forehead and drags it in a diagonal trail of bright light to his brow. He adds a second diagonal line, cutting through the first, forming a blazing cross on Gage's head and then traces a circle around it. The symbol fades within seconds.

I draw in a sharp breath. "Are you going to kill him?"

"No. What happens to him isn't my decision to make. I was tasked with finding him and taking him back."

"Back? Where?" I ask, still breathless and trembling.

Matthew answers with a silent stare. He bunches Gage's shirt in his fist. "I have to go now, Kim."

"You can't." I'm aware of the desperation in my voice. "Matthew, please don't leave me alone." After what Gage did, I need to feel safe. I need someone I can talk to and Matthew is the only person who knows the truth.

"I can't stay. My duty…"

"Please."

Regret fills his eyes. "I'm sorry, Kim. I can't."

He stumbles to his feet, pulling Gage with him. He stares upwards and traces a shimmering 'l' in the air. Beside it, he traces a 'j' and in-between, he pulls his fingertip down in two short gestures. As the symbol shivers and dissipates, bitter wind fills the room, freezing the tears on my face. I look upward at the intense whirlpool of light engulfing my ceiling.

"It's over, Kim."

The light descends, encasing Matthew and Gage. It becomes brighter and brighter, forcing me to cover my eyes with my hands.

The wind and light are sucked from the room in a massive rush, making my ears pop and my skin crackle. I don't need to look to know I'm alone. I press my hands against my eyes, allowing tears to wrack my body. Matthew is wrong. It isn't over.

*

It's dark outside. My room is softly illuminated by the streetlamp on the opposite side of the road. I pick myself up from the floor and drag my palms over my face to wipe the tears away. My quivering legs can barely hold my weight, but I manage to stumble into the bathroom and clamber into the shower. It's only when the hot water is thundering over my head and shoulders I realise I'm still fully dressed. I drag the drenched T-shirt over my head, and hurl it to the floor. I push the jeans from my legs, leaving my thighs pink and rip my bra and knickers off. Everything lands in a soggy pile. Then I squeeze a generous dollop of shower gel onto my hands and wash Gage's touch from my skin.

I get out and grab a towel, rubbing at my flesh with the scratchy fabric. I can still feel Gage's fingertips easing their way over my body. I shudder and choke back a sob.

I walk as though in a daydream to my room and tug on clothes that Gage hasn't polluted. I head to the wardrobe and pull out a large roll of posters. I don't care which ones I grab. None of them have graced my walls in a couple of years. They're a reminder of my boy band fetish. I knead blu-tack between my fingers and stick generously sized blobs to the corners of a poster.

I hesitate as I approach the wall. I can't tear my gaze away from the thin cracks in the plaster. I hope Matthew is all right.

I hang the poster on the wall, pressing longer than necessary to make sure it sticks. It isn't big enough, so I repeat the process again, creating a collage of my past to hide the secrets of the present.

It's then I notice the cold air pouring through the open window. I slam it shut and turn the lock. Rubbing my upper arms, I turn to face the room, shivering.

I spot the crumpled remnants of Gage's phone. I gather up the wreckage and the damp clothes from the bathroom floor. I intend to go downstairs, into the kitchen, but I find myself standing in Charley's room instead.

Everything is so perfect and neat. I clench my teeth so hard my face aches with anger. Charley must have known what kind of monster Gage was. Why didn't she warn me? The damp clothes and crushed phone tumble from my arms. Mind numb,

I step over them and trudge to her wardrobe. The first thing I see when I fling the white doors open is her peach ball gown. It's safely cocooned in a dry-cleaning bag, but the sequins still shimmer in the light from the hallway. Gage danced with her the night she wore the dress. He held her hand. Linked arms with her. Did he touch her? Kiss her? Caress her? Seduce her?

I wrench the dress off the hanger. I drag it out of the bag, not caring when I hear the quiet hiss of ripping plastic. The dress rustles in my arms. I clench the sleeves in my fists, scream through my gritted teeth and pull. The fabric screeches as it tears.

"This is all your fault," I yell.

The organised perfection of Charley's room stares back at me, taunting me. I rip the dress downwards, splitting it from neck to waist. Sequins tumble to the carpet and wink up at me cheerfully, fuelling my anger.

"You should have told me."

My hands ache as I tear the skirt. The silk gives in to my rage easily.

"You should have warned me."

Clutching the tattered remnants of the dress in my arms, I sink to the floor. I press the fabric to my face. My tears soak through the cool silk, creating dark blotches, which makes the fabric look like rotting fruit. It's just like my memories of Charley. Spoiled. Forever ruined by the way she died. By Gage.

Hiccups take over my tears, as guilt replaces my anger. I lower the dress to my lap and stare at it miserably. I sat in this room, watching her get ready for her prom. Mum paid for her to have her hair and make-up done professionally. I'd helped her zip her dress up. *"You can tell men design girls' clothes,"* she'd grumbled. *"A woman would make sure she could do the zipper up herself."* She'd smiled and stared at herself in the mirror, turning around slowly, gazing over her shoulder. *"How do I look?"* Beautiful.

But now the dress lies in tatters in my arms. Sequins are scattered on the carpet. It's destroyed beyond repair.

Outside, I hear the rumble of an engine as a car pulls up onto the drive. Mum must be home. I choke on my guilt and gather up the evidence.

I dash downstairs, pausing to scoop up my discarded coat and hang it on a hook. I freeze. Charley's coat hangs beside mine. A sense of déjà vu taunts me, but a chorus of slamming doors pulls me back to the moment.

Everything—the phone, my clothes, Charley's dress—gets stuffed into a black bin bag, which I chuck in the outside bin. But my feet won't carry me back inside. I press my hands to my face and take several deep breaths, quelling the desire to cry or throw up. I push all thoughts of Gage away, but one question remains. Why?

Just as I come back in and lock the back door, the front door slams shut. Two pairs of feet stamp on the welcome mat.

Mum's voice rises above the din. "Hang your coats up. Let's put this food out before it gets cold."

Chris must have brought a friend home to enjoy our customary Saturday night dinner of takeaway. Great, company, just what I need.

Mum flicks the kitchen light on, visibly jumping when she sees me. "Kim, I didn't know you were home." Her forehead pinches into a frown. "Why are you in the dark?"

I fake a smile. "I just got home a couple of minutes ago."

Her mouth twitches and her eyes narrow, but she says nothing. Chris and a tall, sandy-haired boy spill into the kitchen behind her, babbling about some computer game.

I switch my mind off, ignoring their pointless prattle.

"What's for dinner?" My stomach rumbles, but I doubt I could eat anything.

"Indian. That okay?" Mum asks, setting the white plastic bags down on the kitchen counter.

I pull a face.

"I thought you liked Indian?" Disappointment, bordering on anger, laces Mum's voice.

"I just don't fancy it tonight." I move to the bread bin and pull out a half-finished loaf. "I'll grab a sandwich."

Mum watches me as I go through the motions of making a sandwich I'm not going to eat. Under her instructions, Chris darts around me, grabbing plates, cutlery and drinks. I swear he's trying to trip me up. He also "forgets" to get me one, so I help myself.

With my hands filled with a plate and drink, I try to slip out.

Mum stops me with a light touch on my arm. "Are you all right?"

I plaster the same fake smile across my lips. "Of course. Just..." I nod my head towards the boys. "I'd rather be by myself." I don't wait for Mum to reply.

Nor do I go back to my room. I stand on the landing, staring blankly at Charley's door. Grief, guilt and disgust churn in the pit of my stomach. I can't go back into her room. Mum's room? No chance. She'd be psycho-analysing me the second she realised I was there. Then again, she'll do that wherever I end up tonight. Chris's room? I'm not sure why the thought even popped into my mind. The bathroom? I'm clutching at straws now. I look up at the loft access. I can imagine the withering look Mum will give me if I sleep up there, but it's preferable to my room.

I pull down the loft hatch and ladder and climb up into the stuffy space, juggling the plate and glass. I switch the light on with my elbow, revealing a haven for spiders. Cobwebs cling to every beam and corner, fluttering in the draft from the access hatch. Cardboard boxes squat in neat stacks, each one clearly labelled with thick black marker pen. Okay, "room" is stretching it a bit, but it's cosy enough if you can ignore the squatters.

I notice a box marked "C & K's Wendy House." Tears spring to my eyes. Charley and I used to have so much fun shutting each other out of the brightly coloured Wendy House. It was yellow and red with just enough room inside for a pair of toddler chairs and a little plastic table. My hands tingle at the memory of getting my fingers trapped in the door when Charley slammed it on me. I got my own back just as often.

I set my drink and sandwich aside and slip back down the ladder to pull a spare quilt and pillow from the airing cupboard. Exhaustion creeps up on me before I've finished arranging my nest—in the least spider-infested corner. It's a good thing they don't bother me. I'm not sure I want to sleep, but I'm too drained to stay awake. I huddle beneath the quilt, tugging it up around my ears. Embraced in warmth and solitude, my eyelids flutter shut.

My last waking thought is of Charley. Why did she die?

CHAPTER SIXTEEN

Mum stops and stares at me the second she steps through the kitchen door. She takes in my neatly pressed school uniform. Her eyebrow arches as she inspects the collar of my blouse, for once buttoned up to the top with the school tie neatly fastened.

"You're not ready to go back to school." Her tone is flat.

I pause to finish the mouthful of cereal I've been chewing. "I think I am."

Mum's lips press into a thin line of disapproval. "You've been sleeping in the loft since Saturday."

I'm surprised she's waited until Monday morning to mention it. When I woke up on Sunday, she'd laid an extra blanket over me—typical Mum. She must have tried to check on me and found me missing. I wasn't hard to find. I'd left the loft ladder down.

I glance at Chris, expecting him to snigger into his cereal. Instead, he glowers.

"I want to go back to school," I say. I shovel more of the tasteless breakfast into my mouth, chewing slowly. It would be great if this was the end of the discussion.

Mum sits down opposite me. "Have you forgotten what happened last time? It was only a week ago." She reaches her hand across the table.

I shuffle my bowl away from her, so her fingertips can't graze my hand. I swallow the cereal. It feels like dozens of little needles are being forced down my throat. "I haven't forgotten, but I can't avoid school forever." And I don't want to be in the house right now, let alone in my room.

"Maybe I'll let you go back, after a few more visits to the grief counsellor."

I slam my fist on the table, rattling the bowls and cups. Milk sloshes out of my bowl. Chris hunches his shoulders.

"You'll let me? Mum. I'm sixteen, not five."

Mum takes a deep breath. "Then act like it, Kim." Her voice is slow and quiet.

I push my bowl away, unable to face the food anymore. She's right, my reaction was childish.

"I'm sorry." I mumble the apology and then raise my voice as I continue. "But I want to go back to school today."

I'd take maths and double science over staying at home, worrying about questions I'll never get the answer to. I'd take P.E. over having to go back into my room.

I lift my head and stare at Mum with wide eyes and raised eyebrows. "Please?"

Her shoulders sag. She's started looking older since Charley died. Her hair isn't as neat as it used to be and dark bags are beneath her eyes. Crow's feet and laughter lines seem more obvious. It's like she's aged ten years in a couple of weeks.

She nods. "All right. I'll drive you both."

"We can get the bus," Chris mutters.

I stare at my kid brother. It isn't like him to turn down a lift anywhere. He goes straight back to eating, avoiding my stare by glaring at the multi-coloured o's swimming around in his milk.

"I'm going to get my stuff together." I push my chair back before Mum can say a word and hurry out of the kitchen and up the stairs.

I pause outside my room, fingers grasping the handle. My bag, books—everything is inside. I take a deep breath and open the door, part of me hoping Gage's visit on Saturday night was a terrible dream.

I shiver as I step inside. The temperature has to be a couple of degrees colder than the rest of the house. I glance at the window, but it's shut and locked, just as I'd left it. The old posters are still on the wall, although the corner of one has curled down. I use my thumb to stick it back up, jamming the blu-tack hard against the wall. It wasn't a dream. It happened. I stare at the ceiling, where Matthew and Gage vanished in a burst of light. It's just plain old boring white now.

I turn to my desk, pick my bag off the floor and shovel every book I can find into it. I shoulder the bag, realise it's far too heavy and rush out anyway. I don't want to stay in my room long enough to check my timetable and take out the books I don't need. The door slams shut behind me.

Chris and I head to the bus stop in silence. He sets a faster pace than me, striding ahead, forcing me to jog to catch up. The bus stop is empty when we get there. Chris turns round and lands a punch on my shoulder.

"Ouch." I nurse the tender skin. "What did you do that for?"

"Because you're a jerk." Chris's eyes are narrowed. His mouth is twisted into a snarl.

My jaw becomes slack. I have no idea what he's talking about.

"Mum is worried sick about you."

"Chris…" I go to put my hand on his arm, but he knocks me away.

Shaking his head, he turns his back on me and kicks the ground. "What's with you? Why are you acting so weird? Sleeping in the loft. Lying. Freaking Mum out. She thinks…" He pauses long enough to draw in a deep breath and hunches his shoulders up to his ears. "I think…" His voice wobbles over the words.

I press my hand over my mouth.

Chris swings back round to face me. "You're a jerk. You can't do a Charley. You can't do that to Mum and Dad. Or me."

I grab Chris and force him into a hug. He bashes his fists against me for several seconds, before finally standing stiffly in my embrace.

"I'm not going anywhere. I'm sorry I'm acting strange. It's just... I don't think... I don't believe..."

"Charley killed herself?" Chris's voice is muffled by my coat.

I nod. My breath catches in my throat. Does he feel the same way?

Chris brings his hands up and round, knocking my arms away. He takes a step back. "Well she did," he shouts. "So deal with it."

My breath puffs out of me. I glance around at the passers-by who stop to stare. I smile sweetly at them, sending them scurrying away.

"And stop being so selfish." Chris's eyes are sparkling with tears. He brushes them away with the heels of his hands.

"Chris..." The approaching bus cuts off my words.

He sticks his arm out, refusing to look at me. He boards the bus first and when I sit down behind him, he moves and stomps to the back. I don't follow. Making a scene on the bus won't help either of us. I'm not sure what will.

*

Sophie's eyebrows shoot up in surprise when I wander into registration. Her expression is shared by most of the students and our tutor. Ignoring everyone else, I shoot Sophie a smile and slink down into the seat beside her.

"Are you okay?" she whispers, as our tutor starts to read out notices.

I nod, tugging my collar up until it collides with my jawbone. I can't risk anyone seeing the dark bruises, a grizzly choker round my neck.

Sophie slips a glossy folded A3 sheet out of her bag and slides it across the desk to me. I recognise the dark blue banner across the top as the school newspaper. It's the first edition of the year. Beneath the masthead, Charley's prom night picture stares at me, her sparkling blue eyes finding my gaze. I shudder.

"It's a memory piece," Sophie mutters. "It's really nice."

My fingertips graze the glossy paper, but my eyes won't focus on the words. A lump forms in my throat.

"Take it," Sophie urges. "Read it when you're ready. Maybe your mum would like to see it?"

I swallow the lump away. Mum would either frame it or throw it straight in the bin. I'm not sure which. I fold the paper in half, hiding Charley's picture, and stuff it into my bag. A tear spills from my eye as Sophie rests her hand on my arm. She squeezes gently just as the school bell pierces the background hum of chatter.

"What's first?" I mumble.

"Option blocks. English is second, so I'll see you there?"

I nod, hoping I'll last that long.

*

I'm not sure how, but I do survive the day at school, despite the stares and taunts. Not only am I the sister of the girl who killed herself, but I'm also the freak who flipped out in school. I'm not sure I'm ever going to live either thing down.

After lessons have finished, I head to the library. Homework club is on every night after school, otherwise known as the time you can doss about on the school computers.

I punch in my username and password and wait what seems like an age before the desktop appears. I fire up a web browser, another task that takes forever. The search engine is the default home screen. My fingers hover over the keyboard while I force my mind to run over the things Gage said last night to Matthew. What did he call him? Sha-ma-ri. I type the word into the search box, hoping I've spelled it right. At the very least I've spelled it phonetically.

The first link is to a baby name popularity site, which tells me two things: it means "he who is ready for battle" and it isn't a popular name. Big surprise.

Next, I find links to a hair salon, a band and a couple of personal websites. Nothing linked to angels with inhuman strength and telepathic abilities.

I flick back to the name site. It claims Shamari is Arabic. I'm not sure what help it is, probably none. I close the browser down and push the keyboard away, knocking it into the base unit with a tinny thud. What difference does it make what Matthew is? I need to know why Gage killed my sister and why he tried to kill me. I frown. He'd been asking me about Matthew. Then he tried to kill me. Is all of this somehow Matthew's fault?

I raise my hand to my neck and trail my fingertips over the bruises created by the pressure of Gage's fingertips. I've never felt so alone.

I grab my bag and head out of the library. I've barely rounded the corner of the school when someone grabs me and shoves me against the wall. Tia lurches into view, putting her face so close to mine our noses almost touch.

She narrows her eyes. "Where's Gage?"

"I don't know." What else can I do except lie? She'd laugh in my face if I told her Gage tried to kill me with magic and was taken away by an angel.

"You're lying," Tia says, spitting the words. "I know he went to see you yesterday. He told me so. I haven't seen him since and he's not answering my calls. So where is he?"

Apparently, there isn't any mobile phone reception in hell. I marvel at my mind's glib response to Tia's anxiety.

She presses her hand on the wall next to my head. "Tell me," she says, her voice quivering, robbing her angry tone of its impact.

What can she do to me? Beat me up? It's nothing compared to what Gage has already done. It's nothing compared to losing Charley.

"I don't know," I repeat in the calmest voice I can muster. "I didn't see him yesterday." I look Tia directly in the eyes as I lie. I don't even blink. I will not allow myself to feel a shred of guilt for Gage's disappearance.

She thumps my shoulder, slamming my back into the wall. The impact makes my teeth smash together. I catch my tongue and blood drips into my mouth. I fight to keep my face blank. I don't want her to know she's hurt me.

"Tell me where he is," she says.

I push Tia back and stand upright. "How the hell would I know, Tia?" I take a step towards her, folding my arms across my chest. "Maybe you should keep better tabs on your boyfriend. Put him on a leash or something." I'm sick of being pushed around.

Tia squeals and comes at me, hands flying to slap me. I don't put up much of a fight. I let her knock me back against the wall while I raise my arms to shield my face as she slaps and scratches me.

"You bitch," she screams over and over. "You lying bitch."

I feel sorry for her. She doesn't know what Gage is really like. She doesn't know he's a murderer.

My heart seems to freeze. Will anyone ever know?

I catch hold of Tia's wrists and push her backwards, fighting to maintain my grip as she tries to wrench her arms free.

"Back off," I say. "I don't know where Gage is." Which is the truth.

I want to know where he is. I need to know where Matthew took him and what's going to happen to him. He should be in jail. That's what happens to murderers. They don't get spirited away by biblical creatures. I shove Tia's arms towards her body, knocking her backwards.

She trips, stumbling into the road. Luckily it's empty. She steps back onto the safety of the pavement and jabs her finger against my chest.

"If I find out you're lying to me…"

I don't react to her threat. Tia can't do anything to me. Her bastard boyfriend has already done it all.

"Why did Gage and Charley break up?" I ask.

Somehow, I don't think it's because he really fancied me. I shudder at the memory of his seductive lie. My question stuns Tia into wide-eyed silence.

"Why did Gage hate Charley?"

My second question causes Tia's jaw to drop. She snaps her mouth shut and shakes her head. The corners of her mouth curl into a cruel smile.

"Because she was a backstabbing bitch. Who wouldn't hate her?" She knocks my bag to the floor, spilling the contents onto the ground, before turning on her heel and stalking off down the road.

I don't watch her go. Whatever Gage has told her about Charley is a lie. I crouch down and stuff my belongings back in my bag. The school newspaper flaps open and closed, allowing Charley's photograph to taunt me again. I pick it up and stare at the memory piece. A plan forms in my mind.

Standing, I flex my arms. The weight of Tia's blows is still heavy upon them. I'll probably develop another set of bruises to match the ones on my neck.

*

I walk round to Amy's straight from school, using Charley's mobile phone to find the address. It's on a quiet cul-de-sac. Every house is an identical box, set back from the road, with neat gardens and gravelled driveways.

I hesitate before knocking on her door. What am I doing here? I push my doubt away. I need answers. If I'm the only one who will ever know Amy was murdered, I owe it to her to find out why. I breathe out slowly. I can't ignore the sick feeling in the pit of my stomach.

The decision is taken out of my hands, when a powder blue family car pulls into the drive, its wheels crunching on the gravel. A pale-faced woman gets out, pulling a canvas bag of shopping out with her. Her expression pinches into a frown as she sees me.

"Can I help you?"

We stand there staring at each other. This has to be Amy's mum. Mrs. Johnson has dark bags beneath her eyes. Her greying brown hair is tied back messily and her clothes look like they've been slept in.

Finally, I find words, another lie. "I'm writing a piece on Amy for the school newspaper. I was wondering if I could talk to you about her?"

Mrs. Johnson's chin quivers. She shakes her head, dislodging tiny tears that splatter to the ground, and then pushes past me to jam her key into the lock.

"I'm Charley's sister," I say in a louder, braver voice. "Please? I'd just like to talk to you."

She pauses and leans her forehead against the door. After taking a few deep breaths, she turns to face me again.

"Charley's sister?" She looks dazed, like she's just woken up.

I nod and stick my hand out as I step up to her. "Kim Welles."

She stares blankly at my hand, blinking repeatedly.

"I'm really sorry," I whisper, dropping my arm to my side. "I know it probably makes no difference to you, but I'm sorry about what happened to Amy." I mean it, I really do. A voice inside me thinks her death was partly my fault. She was meeting me. She'd wanted to tell me something and then Gage killed her.

"Come in." Mrs. Johnson pushes the door open and makes her way through to the kitchen. "Do you want a coffee?"

I shake my head. "No thanks."

She begins to put things away, opening cupboard doors and the fridge and freezer mechanically. I leave her to it and stare at the room. Amy's kitchen is more homely than mine. The cupboards are all made from warm wood. Brightly coloured tiles form a splash-back behind a fake range cooker. The walls are painted pale terracotta and adorned with photos of far-flung destinations, each labelled with a month and year.

"Did you take these?" I ask.

Mrs. Johnson follows my gaze and nods. She fills the kettle with water and flicks it on. Then grabs a couple of hand-painted mugs out of a cupboard. One says "Mum" on it in bright orange and has a massive painted daisy. The other says "Amy" and has a significantly better painting of a white cat with a red collar on it.

"No thanks, Mrs. Johnson, no coffee for me," I remind her in as casual a voice as I can.

Amy's mum pulls a jar of coffee and a pot of sugar out of a high cupboard. I scan the room again and spot a pair of cat bowls on the floor near the back door. One of the bowls is labelled water. The other says "Mogget." My gaze tugs back to the painting on Amy's mug. White cat, red collar, "Mogget." I can't help but smile at the Garth Nix reference. I wonder who was the fan, Amy or her mum?

The bubbling kettle draws my attention back to Mrs. Johnson. She pours water into the two cups.

"Milk? Sugar?"

"No, thanks. I don't like coffee."

She sets the kettle down and adds two spoonfuls of sugar to each cup and a generous serving of milk. She stirs them simultaneously, the spoons clanking around the ceramic mugs noisily.

"Let's go into the sitting room," she says, handing me a mug. "It's more comfortable in there."

I follow her through without a word, cradling the hot mug in my hands. My nose wrinkles at the strong smell.

She's right. The sitting room is more comfortable. A massive corner sofa takes up most of two walls, and a huge armchair you could probably get lost in. In the corner opposite the sofa, a large TV hangs on the wall. An enormous glass coffee table dominates the center of the room. Everything is oversized, making the room comfortably full.

Mrs. Johnson sits down on the sofa, picks up a remote and turns the TV on. The volume is turned down low, providing a background hum. I sit down in the armchair. It's impossible for me to sit back and still balance the coffee mug, so I perch on the edge. My legs shake nervously. Mrs. Johnson buries her gaze in her milky coffee, leaving me to stare at the photos on the wall.

They're all of Amy and some of them include her mum, too. Amy at school. Amy in a play. Amy on holiday. My stomach churns at the sudden realisation that I'm lucky. I might have lost Charley, but I still have Chris and Mum and Dad. Mrs. Johnson has no one. I stare at the coffee I'll never drink. I doubt she'll even notice.

"I wanted to ask if there was anything you'd like to say about Amy, to go in the memory piece?"

Mrs. Johnson nods, but says nothing. I wait patiently, wondering if I should say or do something else. The steam from my coffee gradually fades until it vanishes completely. White swirls of milk settle on the caramel coloured surface. The TV drones on.

Eventually, when the silence gets too much for me, I stand and put my mug on the table.

"Do you mind if I use your toilet?"

She shakes her head but doesn't offer to tell me where it is. I hurry out of the room, glad to be on my own. Relief floods through me that Mum is able to hold it together, that she hasn't turned into a walking zombie like Mrs. Johnson. I head up the stairs. The only reason Mum hasn't crumbled completely is because of me and Chris. She needs us as much as we need her, maybe even more now Charley is gone.

It isn't hard to work out which room is Amy's. It's the only one with the door shut. I glance down the stairs. I can see the open sitting room door clearly, but there's no sign of her mum. I open Amy's door and step inside.

It's exactly like walking into Charley's room. Left as it was before Amy died, down to a dirty jumper on the floor that missed the wicker laundry basket. I scan the room quickly, worried her mum will come up the stairs looking for me at any moment. Amy's room is far more girly than Charley's. She has pink gingham curtains that match her bedspread, a white dressing table, with matching chest of drawers and wardrobe. A white Apple computer is perched on a desk. Posters of horses line the walls and a host of red rosettes are pinned along the top of the headboard. She must have been a talented rider to win so many events.

I rummage through her desk drawers, unsure what I'm looking for. All I find is cute stationary and revision books. I turn my attention to her dressing table. The first drawer is full of makeup and perfume. Heat rises to my cheeks as I open the second drawer to find an array of delicate underwear. When I open the final drawer, I hit the jackpot.

A scrapbook with a hand-decorated cover sits at the bottom. I lift it out, running my fingers over the pale pink ribbons and glittering lilac sequins. The scrapbook creaks when I open it, revealing pictures of Amy and her friends. As I leaf through each page, I discover Charley features in most of the photos, often taking pride of place in the center. My brow creases into a frown. Another familiar face is in all of the early photos, Tia. But then she's gone.

Amy, miss super organised, dated every chronologically ordered photograph. I trace my finger beneath the date of the last photograph that featured Tia. February. Nine months ago. My frown deepens and I chew the inside of my cheek, trying to recall what happened last February. Then it hits me. It's when Charley and Gage split up.

After putting the scrapbook back, I head back down the stairs, preparing an excuse for taking so long. I needn't have bothered. Mrs. Johnson is sitting on the sofa, staring at her full mug of coffee, exactly how I left her.

I clear my throat. "I'll be going now."

She glances up at me and her entire face crumples. Her shoulders sag and shake, as tears flood down her face. Her hands shake so violently, coffee slops over the rim of the mug, sloshing onto her hands. Gulping, I hurry over to her and relieve her of the mug. The coffee is lukewarm at best, but has left pale brown stains on the otherwise pristine white carpet. I set the mug down on the glass table beside mine and then sit next to Mrs. Johnson. I wrap my arm around her. She slumps against me, burying her face in my shoulder.

"Why?" she whispers. "Why did I have to lose her?"

My hands go clammy and lead lines the pit of my stomach. I hug her more tightly but say nothing, letting her violent tears soak through my coat and jumper. I don't know why, but I'm determined to find out.

*

I sit on the edge of my nest in the loft, cradling my phone in one hand. When the screen fades, I revive it with a swipe of my thumb and stare at Tia's number once more. It took four phone calls to Charley's friends to track down her number, but I'm not sure I've got the guts to dial it. I have no idea what I'll say to her. I'm not sure that, "Hi, are you the reason Charley and Gage split up?" is a good opener. Anyway, the more I think about it, the more that scenario doesn't make sense. If Gage left Charley for Tia, he would have no reason to hate her enough to kill her. Or Amy. I flop back onto the duvet. Where do magic and angels fit into all of this?

A spider drops into my peripheral vision, spinning round on a delicate silver strand. It seems impossible something so fine could support even the tiny weight of a spider. I slide up onto my elbow and stare at the little creature. It twitches its legs and then ascends, back to its glistening web.

I drop my shoulder and fall back again. My pillow poofs up around my head. Angels. Magic. A nagging doubt is still in my mind that I'm going totally insane. Except Gage is missing and my neck is so badly bruised it hurts to swallow.

I lift my phone again, but before I can hit the dial button it rings, overriding the screen. I frown when Kevin's name pops up. The ringtone I assigned to him is the Transformers' theme tune. It seemed fitting. I slide to answer and hesitantly hold the phone to my ear.

"Kim?" His voice sounds a little high pitched.

"Hi, Kevin. Are you okay?"

"Yeah, of course." He doesn't sound okay. "I just wanted to ask you if you've seen Gage."

I scowl at the phone. "Tia's already asked me that."

"I know. She's going nuts here. For some reason she thought you might give me a different answer. Have you seen him?" he says, breathlessly.

"Have you been running?"

"Huh? What? No. Kim…"

"No," I snap. "I haven't seen him." I'm ready to hang up the phone. I clench it so tightly I'm frightened I might crack the casing. How dare Tia make Kevin call me? As for Kevin, spineless is the first adjective that springs into my mind.

"Tia seems to think he came to see you yesterday."

I twist the quilt in my spare hand and clench my teeth together. I leave too long a pause before replying. So long I can hear Kevin's breathing trembling in trepidation on the other end of the phone.

"If he did he must have come round while I was out," I lie. "I didn't see him. Are we done?"

"Kim…" His voice sounds apologetic.

I almost let myself forgive him. Almost. "I already told Tia all of this when she tried to beat me up after school." I pause and listen to Kevin's breath hiss in. "She didn't tell you that part?"

"No."

"I know she's your cousin, Kevin, but…" I shut my mouth abruptly. It isn't my place to tell him his cousin is a first class bitch. I sigh. "Listen, I wanted to ask you something." I didn't want to ask him anything until right now, but he's on the phone and it looks like he and Tia are closer than I thought.

"Sure. Go ahead."

"Do you know why Gage and Charley split up?" I inhale a sharp breath. "Was it anything to do with Tia, or…" I stop myself again. What was I thinking? I can't mention magic. He'll think I'm fruit-looped. "I mean, could you ask Tia for me?"

During a long pause, I can hear Tia's voice in the background. "What is it? What did she ask you?" I wish she wasn't there.

"No. I don't. Sorry, Kim. I didn't know Charley." His words pour out a little too quickly.

And yet he's been around ever since she died, offering more sympathy than a total stranger should. Plus, if he's as close to Tia as this phone call suggests, he must have been aware of Charley, even if they weren't friends. If he did know her, why has he been lying all this time? My mind swims with sickening conclusions. I don't want any of them to be true. All the moisture seeps out of my mouth, leaving me unable to talk.

"Look, I have to go. I promised Tia I'd help her look for Gage."

You won't find him. My gaze drifts upwards and I try to see beyond the loft roof, to the heavens above. If angels are real, does it mean heaven exists? And hell? And God?

I swallow to moisten my mouth, but my voice is still cracked and hoarse. "I hope you find him," I say. What I really want to say is, "I hope he rots in hell."

CHAPTER SEVENTEEN

I bump into Tia in the school corridor the next day, during lesson changeover. She's coming out of English as I head in. Her normally impeccably tidy hair is a dishevelled mess. Her perma-tan has paled to an unhealthy glow and her eyes are sunken into dark rings. She glares at me.

I stop her from pushing past me by speaking. "Have you heard from Gage yet?" I try to sound casual, pleasant even. I'm not sure what I'm hoping to gain from the question.

Her chin quivers. "You know I haven't." Her voice is more dangerous than the pitiful look on her face.

"I don't know…"

"Save it," she says, snapping. "If I find out you know what happened…" She bites her lip, stopping herself from saying anything else. She bashes my shoulder with her own as she stalks past me.

I shouldn't have expected anything other than animosity. But I wonder if Tia hated Charley because she was jealous. Did Gage still have a thing for Charley? No. That couldn't be right. He wouldn't have killed Charley if he had feelings for her. Besides, that wouldn't account for Amy's death, either.

What did Amy want to tell me the day she died? I pull my phone out of my pocket and scroll back to Amy's text: *You've been asking the wrong questions about Charley. It's who she stopped hanging out with that matters. Meet me tomorrow after school.*

Tia. Charley stopped hanging out with Tia. A puzzle piece

snaps into place, but there's still a jumble of clues to fit together. Frustrated, I step into the door, almost bashing into my teacher.

She stares at me, eyebrows tugged together in thought. "Was Tia bothering you, Kim?"

I shake my head. "I was just asking her about Gage."

Her brow crumples into a frown. "Who?"

I stare at her, not quite comprehending her reaction. "Gage…" I realise I can't recall his surname at all. "He's dating Tia. He disappeared the day before yesterday. I'm sure he was in your class." They all were, Charley, Amy, Tia and Gage. They all took literature. I know they did.

"I don't teach anyone called Gage," she says with conviction.

I gape at her.

"Are you all right, Kim?" She gives me the stare I've been receiving a lot lately, concern mixed with worry. It silently queries whether or not I'm losing my mind.

I'm not. Matthew must be behind my teacher's memory lapse and mine. He must be. Gage does exist. He killed Charley. He killed Amy. I want to turn and run, but instead I nod my head and slip into the classroom.

I want the lesson to be over. I want to track down Tia. I stare at the novel we're reading, William Golding's *Lord of the Flies*. Normally, I'd be interested, but right now I don't care what happens to the boys on their stupid island. I slouch in my chair, hunching my shoulders to make it clear I don't want to get picked on to answer any questions and I definitely don't want to read. Thankfully, my teacher seems to agree I shouldn't be involved in the lesson. It drags on. The endless flow of reading, interspersed with questions, washes over me while I stare at the same page for the best part of an hour.

When the bell finally goes, I'm the first to escape the classroom, ignoring the teacher's loud request for me to wait behind. It's lunchtime, so I know exactly where to find Tia. I march straight into the sixth form common room, forgetting to feel fear or embarrassment. I grab Tia's arm and haul her outside.

"What the hell?" she demands, wrenching her arm free the second we stop.

I glance around to make sure no one is listening. "Why doesn't our lit teacher remember Gage?" I say.

Tia's face blanches. She stares at me for a second and then visibly shakes herself. "I don't know what you're talking about."

She tries to walk away, but I grab her shoulder and spin her back round to face me.

"Yes you do. Gage is missing, right?"

Tia's eyes narrow. She nods.

I stop the person passing us, a guy I don't recognise. "Do you know Gage?" I'm starting to think I never knew his surname. "Tia's boyfriend?"

The guy stares at me like I'm a loon. "What are you on?" he asks me. "Tia's single." He leers at her. "But we could change that."

Tia rolls her eyes. "Push off, jerk."

"See?" I say, once we're alone again. "Why doesn't anyone else remember Gage?"

Tia folds her arms. "What do you know about what happened to him?"

I take a half step back. "Nothing."

"Really? Then why are you asking me about him?" She steps towards me. "Well?"

I hesitate too long before shaking my head. "I don't know where Gage is." At least that isn't a lie.

"If you really don't know anything, you'll stop sticking your nose into something that isn't your business."

It is my business, but I nod anyway. I'm not going to get any answers out of Tia. It's the second time she stalks away from me. I pull my phone out, search my contacts and, with shaking fingers, dial Kevin. Tia won't tell me anything, but maybe her cousin will and I need to get to him before she does.

He answers after three rings. "Hi, Kim." His voice is casual, cheerful even.

"Hi. Listen, can we meet up after school?"

"Sure." His bright tone gives way to a wary one. "Is something up?"

"I want to talk to you about Gage." I don't mention I suspect he's been lying to me since we met.

Stone cold silence.

"Kevin?"

"Yeah. Swing by the store? I'll arrange to knock off early. Okay?"

"Thanks." I hang up and stare at the screen. Two things are clear in my mind. Whatever magic Gage was messed up in, Tia is involved, and so is Kevin.

*

I only have to wait outside the record store for a couple of minutes while Kevin grabs his coat from the staffroom. I follow his lead, as he wanders away from the town center, onto the quay, apprehension dogging every step I take. The phrase, "hostile witness" creeps into my mind. I've heard it on TV more times than I can count. It's how I have to treat Kevin.

As always, it's quiet. I push down the fear fluttering at the edge of my thoughts. Just because Kevin knows more than he's admitted, it doesn't make him dangerous. We lean against the wall, which serves as flood defences, staring at the dark water. The tide is high and the current is strong as the river winds its way to the coastline a couple of miles away.

"I want you to tell me everything you know about Gage, Charley and Amy," I say. I'm not in the mood to be careful with my words.

From the corner of my eyes I see Kevin's mouth twitch into a suppressed wince.

"What do you want to know?"

I twist round, leaning on one elbow. I want to be able to watch his face. "Oh, I don't know. Why Gage and Charley broke up? Why he would want to hurt her and Amy?"

Kevin clasps his hands together. His glasses reflect the light, hiding his eyes behind shiny circles, but the tension in his clenched jaw is still on show.

"You did see Gage the day he vanished, didn't you?" he asks.

I pick at flakes of weathered brick, which is probably all the answer he needs. Part of me wants to continue denying it, but if I'm going to get anything out of him, I probably need to show some good faith. Inside, I scoff at the idea.

"Yes. He came by. But I don't know what happened to him after that," I say a little too quickly.

I tell myself I'm not lying. I don't know what happened after Matthew dragged Gage into a whirlpool of light.

"And you think he hurt Charley? And Amy?"

I stare at Kevin, wondering who's trying to get information here. I guess we both are.

"I know he did."

Kevin's lips part in shock. "He told you that?"

I shake my head and turn away, leaning my stomach against the wall. "No. He didn't have to. What I want to know is why."

"Why would I know?"

I choke on a bitter laugh. "Because everyone else seems to have forgotten Gage's existence except me, Tia and you." I wait a few seconds for my words to sink in. "I don't know exactly what's going on here, but I know it's not natural." I'm not prepared to say the word "magic." "And I know Charley didn't kill herself and that Amy's death wasn't an accident." Even though I'm not looking at him, the intensity of his stare prickles my skin. "I was there, remember?" Unable to resist any longer, I glance at him.

He raises his hand, tips his glasses out of the way and rubs his eyes. "Kim…" He breaks off when my phone starts to ring.

Dad's picture pops up on the screen. I dismiss the call.

"Go on."

"I'm not sure what you want to know."

My phone cuts him off again. Growling, I dismiss Dad's call again.

"I want to know why Gage murdered my sister and Amy."

"Gage di…"

This time I take the call. "Dad. I can't talk right now."

"Mum's in hospital." His blunt statement knocks the air from my lungs.

"What?"

Kevin pushes himself upright, frowning.

"She had an accident in the car. She's okay, just shaken up. Can you get here?"

I nod, forgetting for a second that Dad can't see me.

"Kim?"

"Yes. I'm in town. I'll be there in ten." The phone goes dead. I fumble to put it back in my pocket, but my hand is shaking too much.

"What's wrong?" Kevin asks.

I step back, away from him. "Mum's had an accident."

The concern wrinkling his brow looks genuine, but everything about him always does.

I carry on backing away. "If this is anything to do with Gage, or Tia, or you…"

"Let me come with you."

I shake my head. "No chance." I shake my finger at him. "We're not done talking. I want answers. Got it?"

"Call me," he says. "I hope your Mum's okay."

I turn my back on him and leg it down the quay, back towards town. I glance back once. Kevin is standing where I left him, talking on the phone to someone. I don't need ten guesses to work out who he's called.

*

I'm not in a hurry to be back in a hospital. It's not the regimented order, or the scent of disinfectant, it's not even the muted atmosphere. The last time I was here, I found out Charley was dead. The last time I was here, my world fell apart.

I make myself go into the accident and emergency reception to ask for Mum. I'm shown through the waiting room, through a keycard protected door into the treatment area and, finally, into a curtained cubicle. Dad and Chris are sat on blue plastic chairs. Dad is beside Mum, twiddling his fingers. His hands twitch towards hers, but he presses them harder into his lap.

Chris is slouched in the chair, arms folded, face hidden in the hood of a grey sweatshirt.

Mum looks fed up. She has butterfly stitches in her forehead and a nasty bruise on her left cheek. Her lip is bust and swollen. She's attached to a heart monitor and a drip, but she's still wearing her own clothes. She smiles at me and pats the bed beside her. Obediently, I perch on the edge of the bed and give her a hug. She holds me a little longer than I expect, before pushing me away and holding my shoulders. She stares at me as though she never expected to see me again.

"Are you okay? What happened?" The questions burst out of me like fragile bubbles, wobbling in the air between us.

She releases me and waves her hand. "It was nothing. Just a silly accident. I'm fine. Just a few cuts and bruises."

"No one else was involved," Dad says.

"The car looks far worse," Mum says, attempting to smile.

"But what *happened*?"

"I took my eyes off the road for a second and missed a bend." She evades my gaze, her cheeks glowing with embarrassment. "The car ended up in a hedge." Tears brim in her eyes and spill down her cheeks. "It was so stupid."

Dad and I rub one of her arms each, but our actions don't seem to console her.

"Why did you look away from the road?" I ask.

"Kim," Dad says, his voice a low warning. "Your mum has already given the police a statement. Lay off."

"It's all right," Mum says, pushing Dad's hand away.

He scrapes his chair back, mouth drawn into a tight frown. "I'm going to get a coffee. Want one?"

Mum shakes her head.

I wait for Dad to leave before squeezing Mum's hand. "Mum? What happened?"

"I think the car stereo must have a fault," Mum replies. "This horrid music started playing so loud I couldn't concentrate. I tried to turn it off and couldn't. I thought I was turning the wrong knob, so…" She sighs.

"You looked and went off the road?"

She nods.

My mouth has gone dry and there's a sinking feeling in the pit of my stomach.

"What kind of music?"

She shrugs. "That horrible pounding music. You know, the stuff that's all beat and no substance."

I love Mum, but she's really clueless when it comes to music. "Dance music?"

"The rubbish they play in nightclubs, yes." She sinks back against the plastic coated pillow. "I feel so stupid."

I rub her shoulder. "It was just an accident, Mum."

Except it wasn't. Someone did this to her. Tia or Kevin. Maybe both of them. It must be some kind of warning. I tell them what happened to Gage, or they hurt my family. I shudder. I have no idea how far they'll go.

Mum begins to cry. She presses her hand over her eyes and sobs. Chris slouches further against his chair. I reach forward and give Mum another hug, holding her while she cries onto my shoulder. My memory flashes back to Amy's Mum and the despair in her tears.

I'm relieved when Dad reappears with two beige plastic cups of coffee. He sets them both down on the bedside table. I pull away, letting him take my place. Surprisingly, Mum lets him console her. I edge towards the curtain.

"Where are you going?" Dad's voice is quiet.

"For some fresh air." It's a lie, probably an obvious one. I hang my head. "I don't like hospitals. I'm sorry."

Mum glances at me over Dad's shoulder. "It's fine," she says, smiling bravely. "You go. You'll be staying at your Dad's tonight, all right? The doctors want to keep me for observation. It's nothing to worry about."

I nod. Staying at Dad's suits me fine. Mum rests her head against Dad's shoulder, which is my queue to leave.

My tired legs ache as I sprint away from the hospital, towards the closest church. I need answers and right now I'm not brave enough to call Kevin or Tia to scream accusations. Not until I'm sure I've got my facts straight.

I slam into the heavy wooden door of the church, rattling the door knob. It's locked. Of course it is. Why wouldn't it be? It's not the right time of day for a mass and who'd be stupid enough to leave a church unlocked, when anyone could walk in and steal or break stuff?

I sink down on the cold stone step and put my head in my hands. I repeat Matthew's name over and over in my mind and then begin to say it out loud. I might not be in the church, but I am on hallowed ground. Surely, he has to hear me? An angel has to hear me.

I remember Gage laughed at me when I called Matthew an angel, but I still have to try. I don't know what else to do.

My bottom and legs begin to ache from the cold. My teeth start to chatter, slurring my voice. I try to carry on repeating Matthew's name, even though the sun has set and the darkness is gathering around me. Even though I'm scared and upset and angry. I say his name, but eventually I have to admit he can't hear me, or maybe he's just not listening.

I stand and spin round, thumping my fists against the door. "Matthew," I scream at the door. "I need you. I need answers." I wrap my arms around my stomach and scream his name over and over until my throat is hoarse and tears are stinging my cold cheeks.

I pace around the church grounds, staring in every dark corner, but there's no sign of Matthew. He isn't coming.

I jog back to Dad's, glancing behind me, jumping at shadows and flinching every time I hear the blare of music from a car or house. By the time I slot my key into Dad's front door, I'm trembling and covered in cold sweat.

I close the door and lock it behind me and then turn round to see Dad ambling out into the hallway from the sitting room. The green and blue flicker of the TV is reflected on the open door.

"I thought you'd be home before us," Dad says, eyebrows raised questioningly.

"I just walked around for a bit."

"Do you want some food? I can rustle something up for you?"

I shake my head.

"Chris wasn't hungry either."

I step past Dad and peer into the sitting room. Chris's gaze is glued to the TV, while his thumbs hammer the controls on a games handset.

"This is all tough on him," Dad whispers.

It's tough on us all. I remember how angry Chris was with me yesterday morning. His fear I might vanish out of his life, just like Charley. Now Mum's accident. I almost go in and give him a gigantic hug, but I'm not emotionally strong enough to deal with the inevitable rebuttal and sarcastic comments.

"I think I'm just going to head to bed."

Dad nods and ducks back into the sitting room. I linger in the doorway. The sofa squeaks as Dad sits down beside Chris. He slouches back, watching the game playing out on the TV. Silent companionship, it's what they both need right now.

I slip upstairs and into my bedroom. I flick on the light, gazing round at the room that's not really mine, but also not contaminated by Gage. This is a room I could sleep in, if I wasn't so afraid of what's going to happen to my family next. I get out my phone and select Kevin's number, but hesitate. I don't want to believe he's involved. He's been nothing but nice to me. My chin quivers. What if everything he's said and done since we met has been a lie?

I chuck the phone onto the bed and cross to the window. My hands curl around the curtains, ready to close them. I freeze. Standing in a pool of amber light on the pavement opposite is Matthew, staring straight at me.

CHAPTER EIGHTEEN

Shivering, I sneak out the back door, into the darkness and across the road to Matthew.

"You heard me," I say, grinning up at him.

His brow crumples into a frown. "Sorry?"

"I went to a church and called you. I thought you hadn't heard me but…" my voice trails off when his mouth curls into an amused smile. My legs wobble and my brain goes mushy. I've missed his smile.

He suppresses it quickly. "Why would you go to a church?"

I narrow my eyes, able to think clearly again. "Because you're an angel. It's not like you gave me your mobile number," I say.

"I'm not an angel." His dark eyes sparkle with curiosity. "What made you think I was?"

I scrunch my nose up and tap my finger to my lower lip in an exaggerated manner. "Let me see, the wings were a dead giveaway. Unless you're…" I clap my hands to my mouth, muffling my voice. "A demon?"

He laughs, a lovely deep rumble that makes shooting stars zip around my stomach.

"Angels and demons don't exist." His expression becomes serious. "Kim, is there somewhere we can talk?"

I glance back towards the house. We can't go inside. Dad and Chris would hear us. I don't want to go home, even though I know it'll be empty. I shake my head and rub my arms to ignite some warmth in my body. My lovely warm coat is still hanging up in Dad's house. I can't reach it without him seeing me.

"I know somewhere. If you'll come with me?"

I stare at him closely. Matthew saved my life, but he's never been truthful with me. He's held things back, under the guise of protecting me. I'm sure there's more to it.

He returns my stare with a placid urgency. His expression is relaxed, bordering on blank, but his shoulders are tense and his body looks ready to spring into action at my word.

"Someone used magic to make Mum crash," I whisper.

"I know. That's why I'm here." He holds his hand out, his eyebrows raised in an unspoken question.

I lift my hand, my fingertips falling short of brushing against his. "Will you tell me everything?" I ask. "No holding back? No lies? No secrets?"

The corners of his mouth twitch in an aborted frown. "Yes."

I clasp his hand and allow him to lead me into the darkness of a side alley. My heart thumps in my chest. If he means me any harm… No. I can't think like that. He wouldn't hurt me.

The streetlights at either end of the alley fail to reach us. We're smothered in darkness. Matthew releases my hand. He bows his head and hunches his shoulders. His wings rip free of his back with a sharp tear, shredding his dark T-shirt. For a moment the alley is illuminated by the light springing from his back, nullified when each mottled feather forms. Holding my breath, I glance at each end of the alley, afraid someone might have seen the light show. We're alone.

"You're not afraid of heights, are you?"

My eyes widen as the reality of his words sink in. "Won't someone see us?"

He shakes his head. "No one sees me unless I want them to."

His words set off fireworks of understanding in my mind. The school. The park. I gasp, wondering if he was trying to make me think I was mad, or whether he was just trying to protect himself. I brush my concerns away. I'll get to the truth when we're away from the possibility of being discovered.

I nod uncertainly. "But I'm not an…" I check myself. He said angels didn't exist. "I can't make myself invisible."

"I can hide you."

"Hide?" I narrow my eyes. "You mean make me invisible?"

"No. It isn't the same thing. I can extend my aura to you. If you'll let me," he says.

Why not? In the list of insane things, flying with an invisible not-angel is probably quite low down.

"What do I have to do?"

He grins. "Hold on."

His beaming smile pulls me in, melting away the concerns running through my mind. I focus on his dark eyes and step forward. The intensity of his gaze makes me lightheaded. I trip against him, my cheek grazing his powerful chest.

"Hold on," he repeats, guiding my hands to his neck.

I clasp my fingers, feeling the brush of his short hair against my skin. He wraps his arms around my back, encasing me in warmth that pushes away the crisp night. I don't take my gaze off his. I feel the beating of his wings fanning the air around me. Slowly we rise into the night sky like it's the most natural thing in the world.

Still smiling, his body tips forward. The air rushes around us, while my legs dangle over nothingness. I twist my head, which is a bad mistake. My stomach lurches in response to the view. We're passing over toy-town streets. Miniature cars glide over the thin black ribbon road and insect people scurry to their destinations. Wispy clouds dissipate when we collide with them. We leave the city behind, to swoop high above parkland and fields. The last traces of light have fled the sky. Our bodies dip and rise with the powerful beating of Matthew's wings.

My blood freezes when I realise how much power he has over me. He holds my life in his arms. I don't want him to let me go. I don't want to die. As though in answer to my unspoken fears, he holds me tighter. My mind congeals and my limbs turn to liquid. I sink my head against his bare chest and allow my eyelids to ease shut. I don't think I've ever trusted anyone more in my life than Matthew in this terrifying moment.

I don't realise we're descending until the intensity of the wind changes. The soles of my boots hit solid ground, prompting my knees to buckle. Matthew's firm grip remains. He guides me towards the ground and releases me, leaving me with my back propped up against cold stone.

I open my eyes. A blanket of stars stretches above my head. The moon, covered by dark clouds, takes center-place in the wondrous tapestry. In the distance, a sheep bleats. A stone wall surrounds me. All colour and definition is drained from the landscape without the sun. The cold seeps back in, leaving my body shivering and my teeth chattering. I stand, pacing back and forth with my arms wrapped around my chest. It does nothing to ward off the biting cold.

Matthew perches on the wall. The darkness wraps around his naked torso, hiding the contours of his body.

"What do you want to know?" His expression is open, his eyes held slightly wider than normal as he searches mine, waiting.

I truly believe for the first time he's prepared to be honest with me. I hesitate, running my teeth over my bottom lip. Why now? What has changed to make him open up to me? I hold those questions back, sucking in a breath. The cold air hits the back of my throat, making me shiver.

"Where are we?"

"A few miles outside the city. I'll take you home after we've talked. I promise."

I'm in the middle of nowhere with a relative stranger, but I don't feel scared, even though I should. I brush the thought away and focus on the questions I want to ask.

"If you're not an angel, what are you?"

"Angel, demon, those are human labels."

"But for what? Shamari?" I say, recalling the word Gage used. I raise my eyebrows, hoping it's enough to prompt him into elaborating.

His shadowed face becomes taut. "We were created to protect humanity."

My eyebrows slide even further up my forehead and my mouth drops open. "Protect us? From what?"

"From the Baneem." He ponders my blank expression for a second. "The first creation."

I wheel away. With my back to him, I lean on the opposite wall. The rough texture of the stone is interspersed with damp, spongy moss. I'm not religious, but his words contradict all the Christian and Jewish creation stories I know.

"You're telling me God is real, angels were created after us and there's another race?"

"Three races were made, yes."

"By God?" I say.

He shrugs. "If that's what you want to call the Creator."

I growl in retaliation to the irritating calm of his voice. I twist round and lean my hips against the wall. "And you expect me to believe that?"

He flexes his wings. "No, I expect you to believe what's right in front of you."

I can't say anything. I can't deny I'm staring at the most amazing, the most beautiful, creature I've ever seen. I can't deny he carried me in his arms as we flew through the sky. I pull my hands down my face. This is all too much. Yet I asked. I pushed Matthew for the truth time and time again. I can't run away from it now because it's hard to take in.

"What has any of this got to do with Charley? And Amy? And Gage?"

His mouth turns down in a glum expression. "I thought Charley and Amy were killed by one of the Baneem. By Gage." His mouth scrunches into a contemplative squiggle. "It was definitely the power of one."

Gage isn't human? I grimace and rub my arms, pushing away the invisible memory of his touch.

"What are the Baneem?"

"I told you. They're..."

"God's first creation," I snap, cutting him off. "That tells me nothing."

Matthew shakes his head. "The Baneem weren't just made in the Creator's image. They were each given a drop of His power too." Matthew picks at the moss on the wall. "You would call it magic. Each Baneem has a different magical ability, as unique as human fingerprints." He glances up and waits a few seconds, before carrying on. "They used their power against each other, destroying the paradise He'd given them. He became angry and separated them from the rest of the cosmos."

I frown. "You mean He threw them into prison?"

"I suppose so." His shoulders rise and fall in a slow shrug. "He tried again, creating humanity—His image, but without any power. The Creator hoped you would be able to live in peace." Matthew's gaze becomes distant, troubled. "And for a while you did, until the Baneem found a way to reach earth and began corrupting you with promises of power."

"Why would they bother?" I ask. "I don't understand why Gage masqueraded as a human. It makes no sense."

Matthew shrugs. "I can only tell you what the Shamari believe."

I raise my eyebrows, waiting for him to carry on.

"If they can corrupt humanity and make them disappoint the Creator, maybe He will release the Baneem from their home and let them live on earth again."

My brow crumples. "But Gage was living on earth. They must be able to get out of their prison now."

"Only with the help of a human. They can whisper through the divide between worlds, but cannot cross without your help."

"I don't understand."

He rubs his temple and the side of his face. "Baneem convince humans to open doors between worlds with promises of power. They teach humans just enough ritual magic for the task, but no more." He rolls his eyes. "Often, that's enough to snare them."

I purse my lips, mulling over his words. "So where do angels fit in?"

Matthew smiles. "Shamari," he reminds me. "It's our job to stop humans falling prey to Baneem and to send the Baneem home. It's why we were made."

I stand up straight and take a step closer to him. "But you have magic. Why did God trust your kind and not mine?"

Matthew shakes his head. "The Shamari don't have magic."

I fake a cough. "Telepathy? Mind control? Invisibility? Wings? Liar."

The darkness gathers around Matthew's face as he turns it away from me. "This was a mistake." The disappointment in his voice slices through my anger. "I'll take you home."

I rush forward, before he has a chance to stand, and press my palms firmly against his chest. "Wait. Explain it to me. Explain how you can do all those things without magic."

Glowering, he grasps my wrists and twists my hands away from him.

"You wanted to talk to me," I remind him, narrowing my eyes as his jaw twitches. "You promised you wouldn't keep any secrets."

He holds his hands out, staring at them. "We're not like you, or the Baneem. We're physically manifested souls, rather than flesh and blood."

My eyes open so wide they ache. The cold air blows against them, drying them out, forcing me to blink repetitively like a china doll. He looks real to me and yet… I stare at his chest, but it doesn't rise and fall. I realise I've never heard the sound of his breathing and, when I was pressed against him, I couldn't feel the beat of his heart.

"And that's why you have… powers?"

"I'd call them abilities." He shrugs. "But, yes. Because our souls are completely exposed, we can bend them to our will."

My lips part. "And the downside?" There's always a downside in the movies, why would reality be any different?

"We're far more vulnerable. Not to physical damage. Knives, bullets," he swats the words aside with his hand. "But to anything which can attack the soul."

"Like magic?"

He nods. "We're vulnerable. And if our soul is destroyed…"

"You die?"

He stares at the ground. "Worse. We're gone, forever. We cease to exist."

My knees feel weak. Gage could have literally destroyed Matthew if he'd won. I press my hands against my thighs, trying to take in what Matthew risked, for me.

"Gage called you one of the Changed."

He squirms under my stare, his shoulders slumping as though I've just insulted him.

"You were human once, weren't you?" I hold my breath, waiting for him to deny it. He doesn't. "So you were changed into a Shamari? Like someone gets changed into a vampire?"

He raises an eyebrow. "You read too many books. Vampires don't exist."

I fold my arms. "You want me to believe in the existence of God, not-angels and a whole other race, but you think vampires are farfetched?"

Matthew chuckles. "Well, when you put it like that…"

I allow myself to laugh with him, glad of the temporary release of tension. The smile accompanying his laughter catches me off guard, making my insides melt and my body quiver.

I smother my laughter, clearing my throat as heat rises to my cheeks. "Your smile…"

He catches it and banishes it from his face. Regret tugs at my stomach and a murmur in my heart longs for him to put it back, to never stop smiling at me.

"The way it makes me feel." I can't look at him when I choke out the words. "It's not natural, is it?"

"It's part of what I am." His voice is tinged with sadness.

I raise my eyebrows. "Did you choose to become Shamari?"

"Yes."

I shiver at his snapped response. It's time for a change of subject.

"Why was it up to you to stop Gage?" I ask.

"I told you, it's our job to protect humanity from the Baneem.

A job that isn't made any easier by the humans' desire for forbidden power." The bitterness in his voice makes me shiver. He lowers his head. "This area is under my protection. Amy shouldn't have died. I should have been able to track down the source of the magic that killed your sister."

I take another step forward. "Why weren't you able to?"

Tension ripples across his strong shoulders. "I'm not sure why, or how, but the person doing the magic wasn't there. The magic wasn't..." His eyes roll upwards for a second. "It wasn't fresh."

I raise my eyebrows a little, prompting him to clarify his statement.

"I couldn't work it out until Gage attacked you and I heard the music he was playing on his..." He frowns.

"Mp3 player?"

Matthew nods. "Somehow, the magic was in the music. Which means Gage could have given the twisted song to anyone. You need to know something, Kim." He lays his palms on his thighs and stares at them. "My superiors questioned Gage. He didn't kill your sister, or Amy."

The breath is squeezed out of my constricting lungs. Deep down, I guessed that was what he wanted to tell me.

"I'm sorry, Kim. Removing Gage should have been the end of it. But I'm pretty sure the person behind the killings is human, which means there's nothing I can do." Matthew's hopelessness and guilt makes the air between us heavy.

"Why not? Why can't you do anything?"

He stares upwards. "I'm charged with protecting humans, but I can't intervene when they're hurting one another."

"Even when magic is involved?"

"I'm sorry." He pins me under the weight of his unhappy gaze. The clouds roll back from the moon, bathing his body in pale, milky light. I can see the slump of his shoulders and the pain in his face.

I hop onto the wall, gripping the crumbling stone in my hands. "But it's not over, is it?"

He shakes his head. "When I felt the magic used on your mother, I came as quickly as I could."

I frown. "Even though you can't intervene?"

His body stiffens. "I was worried about you."

I turn my face away from him. A smile tugs at my lips, but the gravity of Matthew's words is as powerful as having my face dunked in ice-cold water.

"So that's it? Because it's a human they get away with it?"

"Yes."

"That's not good enough." I thump my fist against the stone, biting my lip to ward off the dull pain radiating through my hand. "You can't do anything, but I can."

"Kim…"

"I can't let this go, Matthew. Mum could have died today, but I can't do anything about it without your help."

He shakes his head. "I already told you, I can't."

"But you can protect me while I figure this out." I stare at him, waiting for him to agree. I stand and stalk over to him, prodding him in the chest. "Or you can fly away and stick your head in the sand, knowing I'll keep digging until I stop them or I'm killed." I shudder at the thought. I hope it wouldn't come to that.

"You're playing a dangerous game, Kim. Most of my kind would walk away."

I lay my hand on his shoulder. "Would you?"

"No."

"You'll protect me?" My hope hangs on the air between us, fragile and almost breaking until the moment he disrupts the silence.

"You know who it is, don't you?" he asks.

I press my lips together. It wasn't the response I was hoping for. "I have a good idea, yes." It has to be Tia.

"If I did help you, how do you plan to deal with whoever you think is responsible?" He tilts his head to the side and raises his eyebrows.

I hadn't thought so far ahead. "We can't go to the police.

They'd think I was nuts." I shrug. "I'd have to find a way to stop her myself."

"How? Would you kill her?"

I gape at him, horrified he could think I'm capable of murder. And yet… "She has to pay for what she's done. She can't get away with killing Charley and Amy." Tears gather in my eyes. "She can't be allowed to kill again." Why can't there be a simple answer? I clench my hands into tight fists. "I'll find a way to stop her without killing her, I swear." I lift my chin. "Will you help me?"

He remains motionless and silent for a few seconds, looking at the dark sky stretching above us. "All right."

A grin spreads across my face, hiding the fear coiling in the pit of my stomach.

"But I can't help you hurt another human, not even a murderer." He looks me in the eye. "Understood?"

I'm not sure I care about the stringent rules he has to follow, but he does.

"You can start by unlocking my memories."

He shakes his head. "I can't. Besides, what good would it do? You already have a suspect. I promise you, there are no clues hidden in your memory. All you'll find is horror."

"What do you mean you can't?"

He shrugs. "My abilities don't work that way."

I open my mouth to argue. Perhaps I'll even accuse him of lying again. And then he smiles, and I'm unable to do anything as my anger towards him flutters away.

"It's time to go," he whispers, as he slides one arm around my back and the other beneath my thighs.

He lifts me, cradling me against his chest. I loop an arm around his neck and rest my head against him. I can fathom out the details tomorrow. Right now, in Matthew's arms, I'm safe.

CHAPTER NINETEEN

I wake to the beep of a text message. I open my eyes, which are surprisingly unburdened by sleep dust. In fact, I feel refreshed. My head is clear, not weighed down by the grogginess of being half-awake. I don't even need to stretch my limbs. Sitting up, I grab my phone. My brow crumples when I see the message is from Kevin. *Hope your Mum is okay. Call me?* Hand shaking, I put the phone back down. Time spent showering and getting dressed might calm me down enough to talk to him. And I do need to talk to him.

I pad to the window and use my finger to twitch back the curtain. My gaze is immediately drawn to the street opposite where Matthew lounges against a streetlight. His stare catches mine and he nods, his lips jerking into a fleeting smile, which makes my anger turn to vapour.

He's still there when I return from my shower. Water drips from my hair onto my shoulder, soaking my dark green T-shirt. I fix my gaze on Matthew while I call Kevin, drawing confidence from his watchful presence.

Fast as ever, Kevin picks up after a couple of rings. "Kim?" His voice is quietly anxious. "Is your Mum okay?"

"She'll be fine." An image of her in hospital flashes into my mind. The look of frustration and anger on her face, the pale quality of her skin and the stitches in her forehead.

"I'm glad."

Is he, really? His voice sounds genuine, but it always does.

"About yesterday…" he says.

"I know Gage didn't hurt Charley," I say quickly, cutting him off. "I was talking crazy yesterday." I'm answered by silence. "Can we meet and talk properly? I promise I won't go off on one again."

"Sure." The hesitation in his voice is painfully clear. "When?"

"Why don't I come to your house?"

Surely he'll be more relaxed if he's on his own turf. This is a conversation we can't have in public and I don't want him coming here, or to Mum's house. Besides, Matthew will be watching me. The knowledge fills me with bravado.

"All right."

"Give me a sec." I cross over to my desk and grab some paper and a pen. "Go ahead."

He rattles off his address. His words are rushed one second and overly slow the next. A few days ago, I would have assumed he was nervous.

"Great. I'll be round in an hour. See you then?"

"Okay."

A dull double-beep signals he's hung up. I breathe out slowly, shaking again. I slip my phone into my jeans pocket. I grab a jumper from the chest of drawers, grimacing at the poor selection. I don't keep many clothes at Dad's house. The only high-necked jumper I can find is raspberry red, with grey trim around the neck, cuffs and hem. At least it'll cover my green T-shirt and the hideous colour clash. Other than hiding my bruises, I'm not going to make any kind of effort for the guy who might be responsible for my sister's death. I pause, my foot hovering an inch off the bottom step. I steady myself by clinging onto the handrail. I don't want to believe Kevin is a murderer, but at the same time, I can't believe he doesn't know anything.

Dad is hanging up the phone when I wander into the kitchen. A variety of kids' cereal boxes and a bottle of milk have been plopped on the table. Chris isn't around.

"It was your mum on the phone." Dad sits down and sprinkles cereal into an empty white bowl. The cornflakes clatter against the ceramic as he drenches them in milk. "They're going to let her go home today." He stares at his cereal, his fingertip idly stroking the shiny metal spoon. "She's going to stay at Aunt Sarah's for a few days."

I lean against the doorframe, watching Dad. His shoulders are hunched. Sleep dust has gathered in the corners of his eyes. He hasn't shaved this morning, so salt and pepper stubble clings to his chin and cheeks.

"I suggested she stay here. I could kip on the sofa, so she could be close to you and Chris, but…" He sighs and shovels a spoonful of cereal into his mouth. A drop of milk misses and dribbles down his chin. He brushes it away roughly, leaving his stubble slightly moist. His disappointment is clear in the droop of his mouth and the slow movement of his jaw, as he struggles to chew the cereal.

I wander over and give him a hug.

He squeezes my arm. "I'm sure you'll all be home together in no time."

But what about Dad? I slide into the seat opposite him.

"I think I'd like to stay here for a bit longer, if it's okay?" My suggestion isn't entirely altruistic, but I don't need to tell him that.

His eyebrows rise slightly. "You'd better check with your mum."

"She'll be fine." I hope. Dad needs support, too. Despite the divorce, I know Mum will understand. "Where's Chris?"

"Still in bed." A forced grin stretches across Dad's lips. "Lucky it's the weekend, huh?" He pushes his bowl away. "I'm sure you've got lots of plans? Hanging out with your mates? I haven't seen Sophie around since…" He sighs.

Normally, I'd love to spend the day hanging out with Sophie—shopping, listening to music, maybe going to the cinema—but I can't until I know the truth about Charley's death.

"I'm going to visit a friend." I refrain from mentioning Kevin. Dad would freak for all the wrong reasons.

"Need a lift?"

I shake my head. Kevin's house isn't far.

I squirm during the following silence. It feels like someone has ripped my gut out, turned it inside out and stuffed it back inside my body. It isn't just Mum and Dad who have grown apart. Dad and I are practically strangers. I scrape my chair back.

"I'd better get going."

Dad's unhappy gaze falls on the boxes of cereals. With the exception of the one he used, they're all unopened. "What about breakfast?"

I shrug. "I'm not hungry. I'll grab something while I'm out." I hurry to leave before he can object but pause long enough to kiss his cheek before heading into the hall.

I grab my coat, pull warm woollen gloves over my hands and wrap a cheerful scarf around my neck. Although the extra clothing staves off the chill weather, it can't protect me from the cold dread turning my legs to lead. I slam the front door shut and glance around for Matthew. He's a short distance away, waiting for me. It's enough to ease the cramping weight in my legs and spur me into a brisk walk.

*

Matthew walks alongside me until we're round the corner from Kevin's house. He gives me an encouraging smile, which cascades through me and fills me with confidence, before stopping.

"Aren't you coming?" I ask. "You said people couldn't see you unless you wanted them to."

He grimaces. "If you're right and Kevin has been using magic, I won't be able to hide from him. Don't worry. I'll be close. Think about me. I'll hear."

Just like he did when Gage attacked me. I nod uncertainly. I'd hoped he'd be right next to me the whole time.

He smiles again, forcing my worry to glide to the floor like a veil. Alone, I round the corner and march towards Kevin's house.

My feet slow to a less determined pace when I reach the address. Kevin's parents are leaving as I wander up their drive. They smile at me cheerfully, before climbing into a dark blue Jeep. They look like they could have stepped off the pages of a department store catalogue. Dark hair, smooth complexions and neatly ironed clothing. I watch them pull out of the driveway and head down the street. When I turn round, Kevin is in the doorway, leaning against the doorframe in a failed attempt at a casual, relaxed stance.

Jumping, I clap my hand to my chest, as if the weak action would stop my heart from leaping.

"Sorry, I didn't mean to scare you," he says. "Come in."

He stands to the side, motioning for me to enter. He's wearing his glasses, a T-shirt with an obscure film logo on and drainpipe jeans. Gel clings to his hair, sculpting it into a spiky mess. Kevin looks normal. But behind his fixed smile, his eyes are furtive and his eyebrows keep quivering, like he's fighting not to frown.

I can't help but glance over my shoulder, even though I know Matthew isn't in sight.

"I'm here." The silky texture of Matthew's voice in my mind gives me the confidence I need to enter Kevin's house.

Family pictures line the hallway. Under different circumstances, I'd probably giggle at the photos of Kevin, which date back to primary school. He was a cute kid. I turn away from the pictures. He's either involved in Charley's murder or knows about it. There's nothing cute about that.

He leads me into a cluttered living room. Knickknacks cover shelves fitted into the alcoves on either side of the chimney breast, as well as the mantlepiece and windowsills. An old TV dominates one corner of the room. The large sofas are upholstered in cream leather and appear to be well worn. The chimney breast has been painted hot pink while the rest of the walls are covered in cream wallpaper with gigantic hot pink flowers. It's not what I'd imagined after seeing his parents.

Kevin sits down on the edge of one of the sofas. He leans

forward onto his knees, watching as I stand awkwardly, gawping at the eclectic mess of a room.

"Sit down?" he asks.

I'm not sure I want to, but I do anyway. The low winter sun shines through the window, catching my eyes and making me squint.

"Do you want a drink? A snack?"

I shake my head. "I just want to talk."

Kevin's shoulders sag. He pushes himself back, sinking against the sofa. He stretches his legs out and drapes his arms over the leather cushions.

"Fire away."

His posture might be open, relaxed almost, but his pale face and narrowed pupils are anything but.

I hesitate. I can cajole the truth out of him or just demand it. Kevin takes the decision out of my hands.

"I don't know what you think you know or what you think I know, but Gage didn't kill Charley. Or Amy."

I blink at his blunt words. They're as clear as if he'd admitted he knows what's going on.

"I already told you I know Gage didn't kill them." I draw in a deep breath. "But I'm sure you know who did." I stare at him, watching for a reaction.

His chin dimples and his cheeks flex. He might as well have nodded his guilt.

I stare at him accusingly. "Who? Was it Tia?" When he stays silent, anger begins to boil inside me. I grit my teeth and clench my shaking hands.

He breaks the stalemate by examining his outstretched hands.

I stand and begin to pace the room, crossing to the window, to the door and back again.

"All this time, when you've been pretending to comfort me, pretending to be my friend…" My voice rises. I'm feeling sick enough I could easily turn round and projectile vomit all over him. It's no less than he deserves. "You lied to me."

He stands, grabs my wrists and yanks me to a halt. I'm left with no choice but to meet his stare. "I've been trying to protect you."

"Protect me?" I spit the words out. I wonder when someone tattooed "victim" across my forehead. First Matthew, now Kevin. "I don't need your help." I twist my wrists away from him. "You're a liar."

Fireworks burst in my mind as chains of logic slot together.

"Gage came to see me after I told you someone made me forget finding Charley." I edge backwards, away from him. "He came to kill me because of information you fed him."

It's the only explanation. Gage wanted to know who stole my memories. He wanted to know about Matthew.

"You haven't been trying to protect me. You set me up."

Kevin shakes his head emphatically. "It wasn't like that, Kim." His expression falls, his mouth sags open. "Gage tried to kill you?" His eyes dance with shock and fear.

"You didn't know?" I narrow my eyes and take another step back, towards the window.

Kevin clenches his short hair in his fists. "Of course I didn't." He breathes in and out heavily. "Look, you're right. I did tell Gage about your memory loss theory. I thought you'd get left alone if they realised you weren't a threat."

"It wasn't a theory and Gage knew it." I shake my head in frustration. "They? Gage *and* Tia?" I cross my arms in reaction to his silence. "Gage came straight to mine and…" I can't tell him what happened. "And it was your fault."

"I didn't know. I didn't think." He stares at me with wide, frightened eyes. "Kim, you have to believe me."

I don't want to. The tension coiling in every muscle in my body screams at me to doubt his words, but the sincerity in his voice runs deep. The panic in his eyes is too genuine to be fake. The remorse crinkling around his mouth is heart-breaking.

He back peddles and practically falls onto the sofa. He nods and then tips his head into his hands. "Oh God. This is all such a mess."

I grind my teeth together. "A mess? Charley and Amy are dead and you think this is a mess?"

"None of this was meant to happen." His raised voice makes my skin go cold. "It wasn't meant to hurt anyone."

"It?" I edge closer and drop my voice to a low whisper. "You mean the magic?"

Trembling visibly, he lowers his hands and raises his eyes to meet my stare.

"I know it's in the music," I say. "It was playing when Amy walked in front of a car. It was playing when Gage almost convinced me to hang myself. It was playing when Mum crashed." I've closed the gap between us while I've been talking. Now, standing over him, I'm shaking as much as he is. "And if it wasn't you or Gage who killed Charley and Amy and tried to hurt Mum, it must have been Tia." I stare at him, daring him to deny it.

He doesn't. His eyes well up with tears. "She's sick," he mutters, his voice quivering. "The magic. She's obsessed with it. It's made her sick."

I expect him to say, "It's not her fault." He doesn't sink so low.

I kneel down in front of him, close but not touching. "Why did she kill Charley and Amy?"

Kevin knocks his thumbs together. His silence drives me crazy within seconds.

"Please. I need to know. Or would you rather I confronted Tia?"

His body shudders. "You can't do that."

"I can and I will, unless I don't have to."

"You don't know what she'll do."

I raise an eyebrow. "Don't I? I know she's capable of murder. If you really want to protect me..."

"All right." His voice is cold and sharp like razor blades slicing through my ears. "They knew too much. That's why."

Amy's text pours into my mind. *It's who she stopped hanging out with that matters.* "Charley knew about the magic," I say.

Kevin nods. "She was the first person Gage showed it to. But she freaked out about it."

"It's why they broke up."

It feels like a heavy weight has settled in my chest, replacing my heart. My sister knew magic existed. She knew the world we lived in was a far darker and mysterious place than we'd dreamed and she hadn't said anything to me.

"Gage convinced her to keep quiet," Kevin says, sighing and rubbing his hands over his face. "Then Gage got together with Tia and revealed his magic to her. She didn't believe Charley would keep her mouth shut." His lower lip trembles.

The weight gets heavier. Cold ripples out from it, clenching my entire breast in its icy grip.

"How do you fit into all of this?" I ask, my tongue heavy and numb in my dry mouth.

"Tia and I grew up together. We're cousins, but might as well have been brother and sister. She introduced me to Gage and convinced him to teach me the magic as well. It was fun and exciting."

"And deadly."

"It's addictive." His desperate gaze holds mine. "No one was meant to get hurt."

"Two people are dead."

"Gage tried to get Charley to come back to us. If she was part of the group, we'd be able to trust her. But she pulled further away. I tried." He grimaces. "You saw how well it went."

I can't breathe. "The day she died, when you tried to talk to her, she wouldn't listen." Her cruel flip-off had nothing to do with a stranger hitting on her. She knew Kevin. "But it was only a couple of hours before she died." My words choke in my throat. "Oh God." I grab hold of his arm and dig my nails in. "You told Gage and Tia that Charley wouldn't listen to you, didn't you?"

Kevin clenches his hands into tight fists. "I didn't know what was going to happen. I swear." Tears well in his eyes.

I release him, push up to my feet and dart to the opposite side of the room. I gulp in air, but it still feels like I'm drowning. Tears squeeze out of my eyes.

"I didn't mean for her to get hurt. I didn't realise Tia would go that far."

I shake my head and wag my finger at him, but I can't force any words out of my mouth. I scream instead. My high-pitched howl fills the lounge and makes Kevin cringe.

"You idiot." It isn't what I wanted to say, but it'll do. "What about Amy?"

Kevin wipes his hands over his ashen face. "Tia stopped her talking to you about Charley." Misery chokes his voice. "She's sick. The magic, she's addicted to it. She can't let it go."

"But why did Tia think Amy was going to say anything to me? She was barely talking to me." I rub my forehead. Did Kevin see the text Amy sent me? Is it my fault Amy is dead?

"Tia said she overheard Amy talking at school, saying she was going to meet you to 'set things straight.'"

Not directly my fault, but if I hadn't been so desperate to prove Charley hadn't killed herself, Amy would still be alive. No. I won't feel guilty for Tia's actions.

I stalk towards him. "How many more people are going to have to die so she can keep using magic? My Mum? Me? Who else?"

He shakes his head and covers his eyes with his hands.

I rip his hands away. "You can't pretend this isn't happening. Tia has to be stopped."

His eyes are liquid with tears. "How?"

His question pulls me up short, which is ridiculous because I should have expected it. How? I've already been through this with Matthew. He can't do anything because Tia is human. I can't go to the police because they'd never believe me. Matthew's words flood back into my mind and I realise knowing isn't enough. Knowing Tia killed Charley won't bring my sister back. It won't bring Amy back or mend her mum's broken heart. It won't put my life back together.

I sink down onto the sofa beside Kevin. "Maybe we can convince her to stop and give the magic up, now Gage is gone."

"She won't listen."

"Then we make her listen." I clench my fists and push them hard against my knees. "We make her." I draw in a deep breath.

"I need to know how the magic works."

Kevin stares at me.

"As a backup plan. It's embedded in music. How?"

He sighs and scratches the back of his head. "I suppose a ritual is the easiest way to describe it. We have to weave the magic into the music as we create it."

My brow furrows. "Create it? You mean play it?"

"Yes."

I purse my lips. "So you can't just sing a song with magic in it there and then?"

He shakes his head. "No."

From the confusion on Kevin's face, I'm pretty sure he doesn't know Gage did. I can still recall the despair his voice made me feel and the physical effect it had on Matthew.

"Let me get this straight. If you can't play the music, you can't make it magical?"

Kevin's eyes narrow. "That's right. But Tia can."

Of course she can. She had a cello when I saw her in the sixth form common room. I mull it over. If I had to, how would I stop Tia from being able to make music?

Kevin tries to touch my hand, but I snatch it away from him.

"Kim, what if you can't persuade her to stop?"

I swallow back a sob. "We have to try." I have to try. At the very least, I have to make her promise to leave my family alone. "I'll tell her what happened to Gage," I whisper. "If she promises to stop."

"It won't be enough, Kim."

I squeeze my eyes together. I'm afraid he's right. Knowing is never enough.

CHAPTER TWENTY

"You're going to do what?" Matthew says through clenched teeth. It's odd to see his normally cool exterior slipping.

"I'm going to talk to Tia and convince her to stop using magic. Kevin is going to arrange to see her, but I'll turn up instead."

I stomp off down the street, acutely aware of how lame my plan sounds, but it's the only one I've got. I wait for him to fall into stride alongside me, watching the way the fine rain that drenches my hair evaporates a few millimetres from him.

"But to do that, I need your help. You have to tell me what you did to Gage."

"No."

I grab his arm, jerking him to a halt. "You have to, Matthew. How else am I meant to stop her?"

He tugs his arm free of my grip. "You know what happened and why. It should be enough. Drop it, Kim. Walk away."

"It doesn't matter how many times you ask me to, I can't walk away."

"You mean you won't." He crosses his arms. "There's a difference, Kim."

My breath growls in my throat as I breathe in. "Fine. I won't. And even if I did walk away, there's no guarantee Tia will leave me or my family alone. She's already hurt Mum."

His shoulders sag. "I'm sorry about that."

"Sorry doesn't undo it," I say.

He rubs my shoulder, forcing my angry muscles to unknot themselves. "Assuming you do tell her what happened to Gage, what makes you think she'll leave you alone?"

I stare at the ground. "It's the only ammunition I have." Honestly, I don't believe she will, but I'm not going to admit it to Matthew. I clench my hands into fists. "It would be easier if you could stop her. She's a danger to humans, isn't…" I stop when his mouth curls into a grimace.

Regret clouds his dark eyes. "The loophole frustrates me as well. If I could stop her, I would, but the Creator's law is final."

"Unless you're Baneem," I say. "Or human. Why do the Shamari cling so tightly to the rules?"

He drops his hands from my shoulders and hangs his head. "If I break the rules, I'll be destroyed."

"Destroyed?" The word chokes in my throat. I hadn't realised.

He nods. "Neither humans nor Baneem face so strict a punishment. You're true creations. We're simply law enforcers." He stuffs his hands in his pockets. "Let it go, Kim. Walk away, before you do something you'll regret." His eyebrows tilt upwards. "Please?"

Anger coils in my gut, as I realise what he's suggesting. I'm not capable of murder.

"I can't walk away." I'm shocked by how hoarse my voice has become. "I can't." My tears mix with the fine rain to chill my cheeks. "Please, Matthew, tell me what you did to Gage. You owe me."

His eyes narrow. "Sorry?"

"Gage started teaching Tia and Kevin magic nine months ago. Why didn't you show up sooner to stop him?"

He turns his face away from me. "A lot of Baneem have been able to get through to earth, Kim. The Shamari don't have the numbers to be everywhere all of the time."

"So what? It took Charley dying before Gage's magic was enough of a problem for you to be sent here?"

"Yes."

His admission feels like a punch to my gut. I step back, shaking my head, willing him to take it back.

Matthew lets out a growl and kicks at the ground. The concrete breaks with a sickening crack beneath the pressure of his foot. I jump back, cupping my hands over my mouth at the stark reminder of how strong Matthew is when he doesn't hold back. Guilt collects in his eyes and his entire body—face, shoulders, stance—droops.

"I'm sorry."

I know he is. I know if he could change things, he would. But he can't. Charley is dead and no amount of guilt or remorse is going to make a difference.

"You can start to make amends by telling me where you took Gage."

His mouth quivers, as though he's battling his conscience. "I took him to the true Shamari. They questioned and judged him. For now, he's incarcerated. Once his punishment is complete, he'll be returned to Uralahnd."

I suppress a smile by pinching my lips together. I'm glad he gave in. I'm not sorry I manipulated his guilt. I have to stop Tia.

"What is Uralahnd?" I ask.

"Their home."

That figures. "Where is he incarcerated?"

Matthew splays his fingers. "It's hard to explain. I suppose the easiest way to think of it is purgatory."

"So he's being punished? That's what purgatory is, isn't it? A place where bad people suffer before they're allowed into heaven?"

Matthew stares at me through narrowed eyes. "Do you want him to suffer?"

I rub my arm and tear my gaze away from him. "Is that so wrong?" I ask in a tiny voice. "He tried to kill me. He taught Tia the magic she used to murder my sister and Amy. Is it so wrong?" I shiver when Matthew closes the gap between us.

He slips his fingertips underneath my chin, raising my head

to meet his dark stare. "I couldn't let my hatred for a Baneem go. I wanted to see her suffer." His voice is quieter than a whisper. "And I'm still paying for those mistakes." He hangs his head. Shadows gather around his face, making his eyes look like dark pits of despair.

"What do you mean?" I whisper.

"When I was human…" He shakes his head. "It doesn't matter. It was a long time ago."

I try to pull him closer, but he remains still as stone. "It does matter. What happened?"

"My obsession with stopping a Baneem got me killed. That's all you need to know." His voice, bordering on a growl, is firm.

"I'm not obsessed…"

"Aren't you?"

I snap my mouth shut. He's right. I am.

"You are exactly the type of person the Shamari would be interested in, Kim. They need people who are obsessed with stopping the Baneem."

I blink. "Need them? To become one of the Changed, like you?"

"Yes. After they die." He touches my hand. "I am asking you to let this go."

"I can't." I release his hand and stare at the tarmac, which has been stained darker by the rain. I take several deep breaths to compose myself, before flicking my eyelids up to give him a hopeful stare.

"I have to protect my family, which means I have to stop Tia."

For a second, when all I can see is the hurt and fear in his eyes and the stiff angle of his jaw, I almost want to follow his advice.

"I have to do this. You can't seriously expect me to walk away now."

Regret clouds his eyes. His cheeks become tense as he clenches his teeth together tightly. "I shouldn't have agreed to help you." He wanders away with his shoulders hunched.

I jog to catch up. "Someone once told me never to live with regrets. You can't undo the past."

He laughs bitterly. "It sounds like good advice."

"But hard to follow," I say. I don't tell him Charley was the one who said it, or that it was her golden rule. She waved away her mistakes like dandelion seeds floating away on the wind.

We walk in silence. I can't help but watch the expression on Matthew's face. It's serious and dark. His eyebrows hood his eyes as he glares at the ground. The tension in his body hasn't eased. I wonder what he feels and how long he's lived with his regrets.

"When did you die?" The question pops out before I can stop it. I clap my hands to my mouth. "I'm sorry. I shouldn't have asked that."

"It doesn't matter."

I scrunch my face into a frown. "What is that? Your mantra all of a sudden? Does nothing in your life matter to you?"

His mouth tugs down.

"Whoever told you the mysterious and moody act is sexy was an idiot," I say.

His genuine laughter pulls me up short. I stop, turning to face him, willing the heat to subside from my cheeks. I'm re-lieved that, despite his laughter, he isn't offering up one of his infamous smiles.

"I didn't mean…" I cover my face with my hands. I blow a breath into my hands, lower them and stare at them. "I need to trust you with my life. How can I do that when you keep so many secrets from me?"

He stops laughing abruptly.

"You don't even like being Shamari," I say.

He narrows his eyes. "I didn't say that."

"You said you were still living with your mistakes, which suggests you hate what you've become."

I take a half-step back when his mouth tightens into a thin, angry line. Maybe "hate" was too strong a word.

"Do you?" I ask. I shouldn't be pushing his buttons, but I'm sick of the secrets.

"No." His voice is so level and calm I believe him.

"Then what did you mean?"

He shrugs. "Exactly what I said. I *am* still paying for my mistakes. This existence… I'm making amends."

"For what?" Getting blood from a stone would probably be easier.

He rubs the back of his neck. "Allowing those closest to me to die." His gaze plummets to the ground between us.

I can't help but gasp at his admission. "But you didn't kill anyone, did you?"

He turns his hands palms up. "I…" He shakes his head. Pain settles on his face like a death mask. "I was tricked by a Baneem. A lot of people died as a result, a lot of people I loved, including my sisters and brother. I watched them all die, before…"

I touch his arm lightly. "Before what?" I hope my voice sounds soothing, but it doesn't soften the creases on his face.

"I swore I'd make her pay for what she'd done, but she beat me to it. Next thing I knew, I was facing a death sentence."

My throat tightens. "You were executed?"

His mouth twists into a grimace. "Strangled and burnt at the stake."

"Isn't that what they did to witches? But surely you weren't a witch? You were hunting them."

He raises his eyebrows and nods. "I was hunting a Baneem. But the irony wasn't lost on me, either."

"That's horrible." I touch my fingers to my neck, remembering the pressure of Gage's fingers.

"I was dead before they burnt me," he says, as though it makes the way he died any better. He grips my shoulders. "If I hadn't become obsessed, I wouldn't have been killed. The Baneem would have left me alone."

I wonder what sort of life he would have had, living with the guilt of the deaths of his family.

"This is completely different, Matthew. They don't burn people for witchcraft anymore, and I don't think Tia is going to leave me or my family alone. She killed Charley because she might have betrayed them, not because she did."

"You don't know she'll keep coming after you. But if you don't let it go, she could kill you. Don't make my mistakes."

I shrug his touch away. "I have to stop Tia. And I'm not making a mistake. I'm sorry you think you did, but we're not the same, Matthew."

Pressing his lips together, he turns and walks away.

My phone rings. It's the tone I assigned to Mum, a classical piece that gradually rises to a crescendo. I'm caught between two powerful magnets, unsure what to do. My thumb hovers over the slider, which will answer Mum's call, but my feet itch to hurry after Matthew. Guilt gnaws at my gut. I've awakened more pain than I had a right to and ignored his advice. But I can't say the words he wants to hear. I take the call.

"Mum? Are you okay?"

"I'm fine." Mum's voice is strained and quiet. "I was wondering if you could help me with something this afternoon?"

"Sure." I make sure my tone is light and bright. "Shall I come to Aunt Sarah's?"

"No. I'll pick you up at Dad's in a taxi. Is two o'clock all right?"

"Yes."

The phone goes dead. I glance down the street, intending on hurrying after Matthew, but he's vanished from sight.

*

It's the first time any of us have been to the memorial garden since Charley's funeral. I stand next to Mum, staring at a golden plaque, which has been staked into the soggy ground. It's stopped raining. Water droplets cling to the bare branches of the trees, reflecting the pale rainbow adorning the moody sky.

"They'll plant a rose bush in the spring," Mum says.

Charley's name has been etched onto the plaque in plain lettering. I can imagine Charley staring down at it, pursing her lips. *It's boring, isn't it?* I roll my shoulders back to hide a shudder.

"It will be lovely in the summer." Mum's mouth trembles. She's still pale, which makes the puckered pink skin around her stitches stand out.

I hold her hand and squeeze it. Nothing I can say will make

her feel better. She leans her head against my shoulder and we stand there together, staring at the boring gold plaque Charley would have hated.

"I don't understand why," Mum whispers. "I don't understand why my baby girl left us."

I bite my lip. I can't say anything. I'll never be able to say anything. A block of ice settles in the pit of my stomach. Cold vapour rises up through my body, paralysing my lungs and throat. I understand why Charley didn't warn me about Gage and Tia. I wouldn't have listened. And now her mini-crusades finally make sense. She couldn't stop them, but she had to channel her anger about their magic elsewhere. At things she could control. Like Kevin's workmate selling gruesome video games to kids. I choke back a sob.

Mum lifts her head from my shoulder. "Kim?"

I realise my grip on her hand has increased, so I let go. Mum flexes her fingers, as her brow creases with concern.

"I miss Charley, too," I say.

Like Charley, I'll have to bury the truth deep inside. Mum, Dad and Chris will never know why she died. Or how.

Mum gives me a brave smile and brushes a strand of hair behind my ear. "I know, love. We all do." She smooths her blouse down, lifts her head high and gives me a determined stare. "Sarah will be expecting me." She turns and heads towards the road, where a taxi is waiting for us.

I linger at Charley's grave. "I miss you so much," I whisper. "But I promise I'll stop Tia." I clench my fists. It's a promise I'll keep, no matter what.

I turn and jog after Mum.

"Maybe you should stay at Dad's instead," I say, once I've caught up with her.

Mum doesn't even look at me. "It isn't a good idea."

"Why not? He won't mind sleeping on the sofa, and you'd be close to me and Chris."

Mum stops, turns and takes my hands in hers. "This isn't going to bring your Dad and I closer."

"I know." But my stomach still sinks into my heels.

"It's best we keep our distance. It'll only be for a few days. Then you, me and Chris will all be back home."

I want to tell her I never want to go home to the place where Charley died and Gage tried to kill me.

"I know the separation has been hard on you." She presses her lips together and sighs. "Do you think that's why Charley took her life?"

I shake my head a little too quickly. "She hated it when you broke up. We all did, but not enough to kill herself."

"Then why?"

I shrug. "I don't know." The lie stings my tongue. "Mum, is there really no chance for you and Dad? It's not like he had an affair or anything." I never understood why they separated. Nothing sordid was going on. Neither of them betrayed each other.

"We grew apart, Kim."

I pull away and stare skywards, blinking back tears. "What does that even mean?"

"We don't love each other anymore."

I shake my head, disbelieving her words. She didn't see Dad this morning. He still loves her, I know he does.

"But you still *like* each other, right?"

Mum nods hesitantly.

"Isn't that enough?"

"No." Her blunt tone quashes the tiny flicker of hope I'd been nurturing since the day they announced Dad was moving out. "I thought you understood."

"I will never understand."

I turn my back on her and take several deep breaths. Part of me wants her to wrap her arms around me and make it all better, but she doesn't and it hurts. She doesn't want to mend our broken family. She can't bring Charley back. She can't make the world normal and sane again.

"I thought I might stay with Dad for a bit longer. He's struggling too and he's all alone. I thought..." I turn round.

Mum is smiling. "It's a good idea, Kim."

My eyebrows shoot up. "Really?"

"Yes," she says. But there's sadness behind her smile and fear in her eyes.

"Just for a little while," I say. "A couple of weeks, maybe."

"All right." Her sadness and fear don't fade. "Come on. I'll have the taxi driver drop you off at Dad's."

My attempted response is interrupted when my phone bleeps. I swipe my thumb across the screen, revealing the text from Kevin. *Tomorrow. Skate park. 10 am.* My breath catches and trembles in my chest. It's actually happening. I'm going to face Tia. Tomorrow. I swallow hard.

"Is it okay if you drop me off at Sophie's, instead?"

I don't want to get her involved, but I need her help with something.

Mum nods and we wander towards the road, pausing at the gate to stare back at the rose-bed containing Charley's plaque. It's odd to think of my vibrant sister reduced to dust, a gold plaque, a rose bush and memories.

"Thank you for coming with me," Mum whispers.

It's impossible to continue to be angry with her when she needs me so much. I loop my arm over her shoulders and hold her all the way to the taxi. Tia might have taken Charley from us, but I won't let her hurt anyone else in my family again.

*

Sophie's eyebrows rise up her forehead comically when she opens the door to find me standing on the front step. She notices Mum, sitting in the taxi and her expression lifts. Grinning, she waves at Mum and tugs me inside. I glance over my shoulder as the taxi eases away.

"I wasn't expecting you. Is everything okay?" She leads me into her kitchen, which is pristine and modern enough to belong in a showroom.

I'm sick of everyone asking me that question. The only way they'll stop is if I pretend I am. Except around Sophie, I can't. My chin trembles. I fold my arms and squeeze my fingernails into my palms to prevent myself from crumbling.

Pressing her lips together, Sophie pours us both a tall glass of orange juice. She sets them on the breakfast bar and motions for me to sit down on one of the tall stools.

"Is it about school?"

I shake my head. "Mum had a car crash yesterday."

She gasps. "I was wondering why you were in a taxi. Is she okay?"

"Shaken up. She split her head open." I trail my hand over my forehead. "She'll be fine."

Unless Tia tries to hurt her again. I clench my fists tighter. I won't let it happen. I take a gulp of orange juice, using the thick liquid to drown the tears building up in my throat.

Sophie rises to her feet and gives me a massive hug from behind. She rests her chin on my shoulder, squeezing across my chest. It's all I can do to keep my tears inside.

Once she's sat back down, I rest my forehead on my hand. "I was wondering if you still have the rape alarm your mum gave you." I know she's never taken it out with her, let alone used it.

Her eyes widen in an unspoken question.

"I used to walk home with Charley every night."

I shift my gaze out the window. Soon, the crisp blue sky will start to darken.

"I hate it when the days get shorter. I'd feel safer walking on my own if I had something I could use to get help, if I needed it."

"The rape alarm does make one hell of a noise," Sophie says, arching an eyebrow.

A high-pitched wail. Exactly what I need to stop Tia.

Sophie runs her fingertip back and forth along the table top. "I can understand why you're feeling nervous." Her words come out slowly, as though she's choosing them with great care. "You've been through a lot. If you want my rape alarm, you can have it." She doesn't move to fetch it. Instead, she stares at me with sad eyes.

I lower my face. I don't want my best friend to pity me.

She sighs. "I'll go get it."

"Then could you go over what I've missed at school the last couple of days?"

She grins and nods. "I have stacks of notes for you. It'll be like you were in every lesson."

I smile as she leaves the kitchen. An afternoon of normalcy is exactly what I need, especially if I really am going to face Tia in the morning.

CHAPTER TWENTY-ONE

The first frost of the year covers the skate park in a glistening white blanket. Even though the low sun is weak, its rays are beginning to melt the frost, creating pockets of shallow puddles. It's too cold to be hanging around, but the dozen teenage boys here are obviously not put off by the temperature. Skateboard wheels whirr against the concrete. Boards clack as they slam down after jumps and stunts. I wrap my arms around my chest and tuck my chin into my coat in an effort to keep warm. At least it's dry. Cars rumble past on one side of the park, while on the other, the river rushes by. It's swollen from the rain. The dark water is crowned by white froth. Sophie's rape alarm sits in my pocket, giving me a tiny shred of confidence.

I notice Tia enter the skate park. She saunters towards me, a cocky smile plastered on her face. My entire body becomes tense.

"Have I been set up?" she asks, tilting her hips. "You put Kevin up to calling me?"

I ignore the sinking feeling in the pit of my stomach. "Yes. I knew you wouldn't come if I asked you to."

She folds her arms. "You've got that right. What do you want?"

I blow a breath over my lower lip. "To talk to you about magic."

She doubles up laughing and blinks away tears. "You really have gone mad, haven't you?"

I narrow my eyes. "I know what happened to Gage."

Her laughter stops and she stands up straight. Her mouth shrinks into a thin, mean line. "Fine. You really want to talk?" She pauses, waiting for me to nod. When I do, she carries on. "Not here. Walk with me."

"Where?" I say, patting my pocket, so I can feel the smooth cylindrical shape of the rape alarm.

She shrugs. "Away from prying eyes and ears." She nods to the skaters, who aren't paying us the slightest bit of attention.

"We talk here or not at all." I fold my arms, hoping it makes me look like I'm in charge. I don't feel like I am. Tia is dangerous and all I have is information.

"Fine." Her nostrils flare.

She jerks her thumb towards the edge of the skate park furthest away from the road. A metal fence separates the park from the wide river. Hidden behind the concrete skate ramps, we'd be out of eyeshot of the road, but within sight of the dozen or so skaters. I don't like it, but it's a compromise I'm going to have to live with. I nod.

The second we reach the edge of the park, Tia advances on me, making me step backwards against the fence. The cold metal digs into my back. I glance over my shoulder at the dark depths of the water. The breeze is stronger near the river. It reaches up to play with the hem of my coat. I push myself away from the fence, standing my ground, even though I angle my head and shoulders away from her angry stare.

"I know you used magic to kill Charley and Amy." I hesitate, waiting for her to deny it, but she doesn't. "If you want to know what happened to Gage, you have to promise you'll never use magic again. Ever."

A small smile tugs at her mouth. "You're serious, aren't you?"

My confidence in my plan begins to drain away from me as doubts crash into my mind. The fact is she could promise and break her word within an hour, or tomorrow, or next week, or… I slip my hand into my pocket and roll the rape alarm into my hand. I can't trust her, but it doesn't mean I will be able to hurt her, either.

I gaze fiercely at the ground. Frost sparkles at my feet. It's an oddly beautiful location to be standing face to face with a murderer.

Sighing, I release the rape alarm and meet her stare. "Do you want to know what happened to Gage, or not?"

"You know I do." Tia purses her lips. "All right. I promise."

I grit my teeth. "You promise what?"

Her eyes narrow. "Don't you trust me?"

I give her what I hope is a withering glare.

She sighs dramatically and places her palm over her heart. "Fine. I promise I'll never use magic again. Do you want me to pinky swear, too?" She holds her fist towards me but keeps her little finger raised.

I curl my upper lip in disgust, prompting Tia to drop her arm to her side.

"What happened to Gage?"

My palms feel clammy. I clench and unclench them, trying to force the words into my mouth. "He tried to kill me. An angel took him away to purgatory." The words rush out in a nervous squeak.

It's amazing how events that will forever be ingrained on my memory can be summed up in a handful of words. She should laugh in my face and tell me how pathetic my "lie" is. Instead she narrows her eyes dangerously.

"An angel? Prove it."

I shake my head. "How do you expect me to do that? Besides, proof wasn't part of the deal."

"Deal?" She snorts. "Did you seriously think I'd really stop using magic? You're either naïve or stupid, Kim."

I stand still, letting her believe that.

She crosses her arms. "Do you have any idea how alive it makes me feel? How wonderful it is to have power?" Her eyes sparkle with madness as she speaks. "I was nothing before Gage walked into my life. Now I can do something no one else can."

I shake my head. Kevin was right. She's addicted to the power. I could almost pity her if I didn't know what she's done. What she's capable of. Tears gather in my eyes. I'm out of options. I have to stop her. My hands feel like they're frozen to my sides. I can't force myself to reach into my pocket and grab the rape alarm.

"They were your friends."

The pictures in Amy's scrapbook flood back into my mind. The three of them happy and smiling, before Gage showed up and destroyed them all.

"How could you kill them?"

Her only response is to curl her upper lip.

"And what about my mum? What did she ever do to you?"

Tia shrugs. "It was a warning to you. And it worked. Here you are, spilling your guts about Gage. I knew you were involved."

"What now?"

I should do what I came here to do. Blast Tia's ears with the rape alarm. But I can't. I'm not sure if it's because I'm too much of a coward, or because I don't want to be like her, but I can't make myself hurt her.

Tia steps up to me, shoving her nose against mine. Her breath coils over my face.

"It's up to you. Now I know what happened to Gage, there's only one more thing I need from you."

My forearms break out in goose bumps. "What?"

"Bring the angel to me."

I bite my tongue to stop myself laughing. "Why?"

Tia wrinkles her nose. "So I can kill him, of course. A life for a life and all that."

"Gage isn't dead."

"He might as well be."

I square my shoulders a little. "How could you kill an angel? He'd crush you."

She pinches her thumb and forefinger together. "Your theory has one tiny problem, Kim. Angels can't hurt humans."

A gasp escapes me, even though I try to swallow it back.

Tia laughs at me. "Didn't he tell you? Bring the angel to me and I'll leave you and your family alone. But if you don't…" She rubs her fingers together as though she's squashing an ant.

I would never betray Matthew.

"Did the angel make you fall in love with him?"

I blink at her, tears blurring my vision.

"Is that why you'd place his life above your family's? Gage told me all about them. They have ways to manipulate poor saps like you, like their smiles. You might hate me for what I've done, Kim, but don't think the angel is innocent. I'll bet he's using you." Her eyebrows angle upwards, drawing together in a sharp triangle above her narrow nose. "Poor thing."

"And what about you? Gage sucked you in, twisted you up and spat you out. Now there's nothing left but a heartless husk, so addicted to magic you don't see anything wrong in killing."

"And?"

The way she stares at me, with her eyebrows raised, her upper lip tugged up at the corner and her weight lazily supported on one leg, makes everything snap into sharp focus. Whoever Tia used to be is gone, destroyed by Gage and his magic.

"Will you bring me the angel, or not?"

I nod. Not because I intend to, but because I need time to think. "But only if you promise not to hurt my family."

She drags her fingertip over her heart. "Cross my heart. Meet me back here tonight, with the angel, otherwise there's no deal."

Stupefied, I stare at her as she strolls away. Exhausted from our encounter, I crumple to my knees. Soggy mud seeps through my jeans. At least my family is safe. For now.

"Kim?" Matthew's molten voice acts like a balm to my frayed nerves. "Are you all right?"

He crouches in front of me, leaning down so I can catch a glimpse of his face. Concern spirals in the darkness of his infinite eyes.

I nod, even though I don't feel okay. "I couldn't stop her. I'm such a coward."

Cupping my elbow, Matthew helps me stand. I fall against him, pressing my cheek to his chest. He wraps his arm around my back.

"It's not easy to walk away, instead of hurting someone. Especially when they've caused you so much pain. I couldn't do it."

I tilt my face upwards, so I can see his eyes.

"What was it you said about not having regrets?" A smile creeps across his lips. "I believe you did the right thing, Kim."

Instantly my insides melt and every fibre of my being screams out that I trust him. I relax into his embrace, pushing myself closer to his body.

He banishes his smile, pressing his lips together so hard they should blanch of colour, but they don't.

"I'm sorry," he says.

My mind becomes my own again the second his smile vanishes. "For smiling? Because it…" I falter, as Tia's words crash back into my mind. "It makes me trust you. Why?"

"It's part of what I am." Sadness creases his face around his eyes and mouth. "A defence mechanism, if it makes any sense."

"Like addling people's minds?"

He nods. I realise it isn't just sadness tugging at his features but loneliness too.

I push myself onto my tiptoes and sweep stray strands of dark hair away from his face. My hand slides down his cheek to trace the angle of his jaw. I allow myself to drown in his eyes. Nothing has ever felt more natural and right than standing with my body pressed against his. I push up a little higher, so my lips can brush against his. His arms stiffen, his body becomes rigid.

"What's wrong?" I say.

His hands slide to my shoulders. Gently, he pushes me so I'm standing flatfooted. He steps back.

"I can't, Kim. I'm sorry." He stuffs his hands into his pockets.

"Did Tia agree to your terms?"

"No," I say, annoyed at the unsubtle change of subject.

The warmth that had seeped into my body begins to ebb away into the ground, leaving me shivering. I hug myself.

"What do you mean you can't?"

"Exactly that, Kim. I can't."

"Is there some rule against it? Are the Shamari not allowed to fraternise with humans?" I rub my face and stare upwards. "Or is it me? Do humans look hideous to you?"

He is the most beautiful creature I've ever set eyes on. Why would he look at me the same way?

"I'm not flesh and blood, Kim." He glances down, his expression stiff and awkward. "I can't feel cold or heat. I don't get hungry, or thirsty." He looks up, brow furrowed, eyes wide. "I don't have *any* physical urges."

Heat blazes in my cheeks.

"I'm sorry, I should have told you."

"Didn't you realise?" I growl through my teeth.

He lowers his gaze sheepishly. "I'm four-hundred years out of practise with girls."

My eyes open so wide they ache. "Four-hundred years?"

"I really am sorry, Kim." Sadness deepens his voice. He releases my wrist.

I stand still, too embarrassed to want to stay in his company, but too trapped by surprise and questions to leave.

"You're right," I say. "You should have told me sooner."

Any anger I might have felt vanishes under the sorrowful intensity of his stare. And even though I know he can't feel anything for me, my body still cries out for him.

I push away my embarrassment and focus on what has to be done.

"I need to stop Tia, before she hurts my family again."

Matthew is wrong. I was a coward for not acting while I had the chance. Promising I'd bring him to her bought me time, but nothing else. I don't want to think about what she'll do when she realises I lied to her.

"Kim…"

I shake my head. "You don't get to try to talk me out of this. Especially now."

If he'd kissed me and held me and desired me, I would have done anything for him, including letting go of my need to stop Tia. I would have found another way to escape her. Found a way to move my family away from her. Instead, I twist my desire for him into protective thoughts towards my family. Holding them in the front of my mind, I stride away. I don't hear any footsteps, but I feel his presence close by, watchful and protective.

CHAPTER TWENTY-TWO

My feet take me home on autopilot. I need to feel angry. I need to gather up all my grief, loneliness and fear into a protective shield so I can face Tia again. I need those emotions to engulf my conscience, to erase the part of me which screams at me not to hurt her. I'll wait an hour. Maybe two. Then I'll call her and pretend I'm bringing Matthew to her. I have to stop her. At least, I have to try.

I stand still in the middle of the street, a few steps away from my front door. Maybe I should listen to Matthew. What hope would I have against Tia? I've already lost the nerve once. And if she's expecting Matthew, she'll have magic prepared to use against him. I won't stand a chance against the magic. But if I do nothing, she'll hurt my family and I can't allow that.

My skin crawls and shivers the second I walk in the front door. It's not hard to conjure thoughts of Gage's body pressing against my back, corralling me to the stairs, leaning over me. My stomach somersaults and it's all I can do to choke back the bile that threatens to project from my throat.

One at a time, I trudge up the steps towards Charley's room. The time warp sucks me in and plunges me into a well of painful memories, which make my head ache and my eyes sting. I curl my hands into fists. Tia took Charley away from me. It has to be all the fuel I need to stop her.

The Transformer's theme tune blares out of my phone, breaking through my dark thoughts. I take the call.

"Kim." Kevin slurs my name in a drunken manner. His voice is almost drowned out by the frantic boom of dance music. "Told you it wouldn't work." Each syllable drifts into the next, as his voice quivers and stumbles over the words.

I frown. "Kevin? Have you been drinking?"

He begins to laugh and then I hear a loud clatter, which makes me jerk the phone away from my ear. When I put it back, only the music is audible.

My breath catches in my throat. The image of Amy's body flopping to the ground pierces my mind.

"Kevin?" I'm answered by a scraping noise. "Kevin?" I shriek his name into my phone.

"Bye, Kim. Was nice knowing you," he says.

The phone goes dead, leaving a humming tone ringing in my ear.

I flee from Charley's room and practically throw myself down the stairs in my rush to reach the front door and escape. Frantic, I sprint through the streets towards Kevin's house, screaming Matthew's name in my mind. My heartbeat thunders in my ears and my breath burns in my chest, as my legs pound across the unforgiving pavement.

A second set of footsteps fall into pace alongside my own. I glance sideways. Matthew's face is relaxed, his pace is easy. I scowl. It must be easy to run when you don't need to breathe.

"Kevin," I pant. "I think…" I gulp in air. "I think Tia's done something to him."

I increase my pace, unable to shake the thump of the music from my mind.

Matthew's arms wrap around my waist, lifting me from the ground. I let it happen, allowing myself to dangle helplessly over the quickly disappearing street. The wind whistles through my ears, creating a discordant soundtrack to our hasty flight.

Matthew sets me down outside Kevin's house. Music pounds into the street, so loud the windows rattle in their wooden frames. I hammer my fist against the front door, but even though I strike it so hard my flesh aches, the sound is drowned out by the deadly music. I try the door handle. Locked. Gently, Matthew moves me aside. He places the palm of his hand against the door, beside the lock, and pushes. The frame splinters as the door swings inwards.

A strong metallic scent floods my nostrils. Matthew tries to enter first, but I push past him and shove open each door I find. The music is deafening and mutes my senses. But I can still smell the metallic stench of the death magic. My head throbs fiercely and every fibre of my body vibrates and tingles in response to the monotonous rhythm.

Every room downstairs is empty. I bound up the stairs, taking two at a time. It's easy to work out which door leads to Kevin's room. An electric blue *Tron* style 'keep out' sign hangs on the pristinely white wood. I throw the door open and freeze, allowing my eyes to drink in the ghastly sight.

An impressive stereo system sits on the floor, booming out music. The speakers wobble with every note. The music sparks a dark desire within me. The hopelessness of confronting Tia starts to crush my will to face her. The weight of Charley's death is draining me. The scent of freshly cut grass explodes around me, dampening the pull of the deadly music.

Kevin lounges on the floor with his back propped up against the bed. Blood runs from slashes on his wrists and drips onto the beige carpet.

A memory flashes into my mind: Charley is lying on the bed, her blond hair fanned out over the pillow. Her arms lay spread wide, palms up. Crimson blood drips from deep slashes on her wrists. Her blue eyes are open, staring up at the ceiling. But they don't see. They're dull, empty.

Dead.

I sag to the floor.

Matthew's touch on my shoulder drags me back to the moment. I snap my head up and stare at Kevin and the shallow rise and fall of his chest. Kevin isn't dead. I can save him. I won't let Tia kill him too. I glance behind me. Dark veins are spreading across Matthew's neck, running up towards his face.

I have to stop the music, for him and for Kevin.

I yank the stereo cable free of the wall. The music dies instantly, but its echo bounces around my body and the metallic stench still suffocates the air in the room. Without standing, I crawl the short distance to Kevin and rest my hand on his clammy, pale face. Then I yank the bed sheet free and throw it towards Matthew.

"Long strips. Now."

He doesn't hesitate. The cotton screeches as it tears at his whim. He tosses the first strip to me and I quickly and firmly wrap it round Kevin's wrist. Blood spots stain the pure white fabric, blossoming out to soak the makeshift bandage. I set to work on his left wrist, ignoring the blood smearing my hands.

Kevin's eyes flicker open and a small smile graces his white lips. "Hi."

I blink at the flippancy of his greeting. I check the bandages. They embalm the grisly wounds, helping stem the flow of blood a little. I hope it's enough.

"Tia made you do this, didn't she?" I say.

"I've been a naughty boy," he mutters, almost giggling. "Think I'm gonna sleep now." His eyelids drift shut.

Tears blur my vision. I slap my hand hard across his face, forcing his eyes to flutter open again. "Don't you dare," I say, snarling. "Stay awake."

"Why are you bothering?" Kevin says.

His question makes me freeze momentarily. My ears have stopped ringing, so each word rips through my consciousness.

"It's my fault Charley died. It's my fault Gage tried to kill you. What does it matter to you, if I die?" He's staring at me. His cold, dull gaze bores into me. Accusing me.

"You don't deserve to die." I mean every word.

"Don't I?"

I drop my gaze from his. "No." Rocking back onto my heels, I fish my phone out of my pocket. It slips through my slick fingers and thuds to the floor. I do my best to wipe my hands on his bed sheets. The sticky dampness spreads onto the sheets, but red still stains my skin. Ignoring the gory sight, I dial 999 and press the phone to my ear. I don't have to wait long.

"Emergency, which service please?"

"Ambulance."

I pinch Kevin's cheek as his eyes drift shut again. When the operator answers, I mumble through Kevin's name and address.

"Please hurry. He's lost a lot of blood. I can't keep him awake."

I hang up the phone and let it slide through my fingers.

"Kevin." I wait for his eyes to focus on me again. "I need you to tell me where Tia is. I need to stop her." I fight to keep my voice level and calm. I hold my breath, expecting him to refuse.

He lifts a limp arm, points and drops it again. "Three doors down." He grins weakly. "You wouldn't think we were so close, would you?"

Fear coils in my stomach. I'd wanted more time to work out a plan. I turn to Matthew.

"Stay with him. Don't let him die."

Matthew shakes his head. "No. I'm not leaving you to face Tia alone." He sets his jaw into a rigid line. "You stay. I'll go. I'll stop her."

A gasp escapes my throat. "No." The word whistles out of me. "You can't. She wanted me to bring you to her, so she could kill you. She'll be expecting you."

I trace my stained fingertip along one of the black veins on his skin. The things he told me about the Shamari flood back into my mind. The strict rules he has to stick to. The fatal punishment if he fails.

"You won't be able to defend yourself against her. And if you do, you'll be going against the Creator's instructions." I shake my head fiercely. "I can't let you." I can't let him destroy himself because of me. I blow a breath out. "Your job is to protect humans. You need to protect Kevin. That's what you have to do. What I need you to do. Don't let him die. Please?"

An internal war twists Matthew's expression into a tortured grimace.

"Please?"

Nodding, he drops to his knees. "All right." The angry edge to his voice sends chills snaking down my spine. "But be careful."

"I will." I guide his hands to Kevin's wrists, observing as he applies strong pressure to the injuries beneath the bandages.

For the first time, Kevin shifts his head to stare at Matthew. "So this is what an angel looks like," he says. His dilated pupils shrink to pinpoints and his expression relaxes into one of serenity. "Wow." His head lolls to his chest.

I shake him, pinch his skin and slap him, but he doesn't wake. I feel for a pulse, not allowing myself to breathe until I find the weak, thready rhythm of his heart.

"Don't let him die."

"I won't." Coming from Matthew's mouth, I accept his words as the absolute truth.

*

I don't need Matthew's supernatural strength to open Tia's front door. It isn't locked. The mournful call of a cello drifts down the stairs as I step inside. The haunting melody makes the fine hairs on my arms stand on end. I sniff the air, inhaling the stale stink of cigarette smoke. Even though it's unpleasant, it isn't the metallic stench of death magic. I creep up the stairs, following the soft melody to Tia's room.

The door creeks open in response to my light touch. Static tingles in the air around my face. Tia sits on a straight-backed wooden chair, cradling her cello between her knees. Her eyes are closed. Her fingers glide over the fingerboard and her bow arm moves swiftly and fluidly. A microphone sits on the desk, hooked up to recording equipment. A red light blinks monotonously, signalling the microphone is capturing every perfect note. I remember what Kevin told me. She must be weaving the magic. Is this the music she intends to kill Matthew with? Or Mum? Or me? Pain blossoms in my chest. I have to stop her.

I don't think as I storm across the room and wrench the cello from her grasp.

Her eyes jolt open and her hands freeze. "You bitch." She fixes her cold stare upon me.

I clutch the cello against my body. "Kevin isn't dead."

She curls her upper lip into a grimace.

"Why are you doing this?" My voice cracks and waivers.

I glance across at the recording equipment. The red light is still flashing.

"How could you kill Charley and Amy? How could you try to kill your own cousin?"

"They betrayed me."

An admission. Recorded. Somehow, I have to get the recording.

"Don't you realise how insane it sounds?"

"Insane?" Tia gestures towards me. "You've got it easy. You and Charley with your perfect little lives. Parents that give a shit, instead of getting wasted and ignoring you every damn day. Gage is the only one who didn't betray me and he's gone."

"My life isn't perfect," I say, "nor was Charley's. And having a crap life doesn't make it okay for you to kill people." I breathe in deeply, fighting to keep calm. I don't want to make her any angrier.

I take a step closer and lower my voice to a calming tone. "Kevin thinks you're sick. That everything you're doing is because of your addiction to magic."

She stands, smiling. I notice her hand creeping towards the play button on her stereo. I knock the cello aside. It strikes the ground with a hollow thud and a hum of strings. A sharp noise slices through the air, followed by a painful twang as one of the taut strings snaps and springs back into a tight coil. Tia pauses long enough to snarl at me, before reaching for the play button again. I launch myself at her, knocking her onto the chair. We both overbalance and tumble backwards, onto the floor. She wrestles me, tipping me onto my back and pins me against the carpet. She clutches my hair in her hands, ripping strands away from my head. Gritting my teeth, I smack the heels of my hands into her throat. She pulls back, gasping. I thrust my knees into her stomach. She grunts and tumbles to the side.

For a second we both lay still, panting.

"You have to stop this, Tia."

"Or what? You'll stop me?" Her mouth curls into a sneer.

Pain cracks across my cheek as she punches me. Dazed, I blink my eyes repeatedly. I'm too slow to respond as she straddles me and presses her hands around my throat.

"I don't need magic to kill you," she says.

I fumble in my pocket for the rape alarm. Black spots saturate my vision. Her fingertips find the bruises Gage left behind. She presses against my windpipe, trapping the remaining air in my lungs. I gasp, choking out a weak croak.

I tug the rape alarm free. It's cylindrical in shape, not dissimilar to a tube of lipstick. My tingling thumb finds the trigger button. Unable to breathe, I bite into my lower lip, allowing the warmth of blood to seep over my flesh, reminding me I'm alive. I won't die. I won't let Tia win. I will stop her. I have to. Trembling, I press the rape alarm to her ear and jamb my thumb against the button.

An inhuman wail shrieks out of the alarm, piercing the air, leaving my ears ringing. Screaming, Tia falls backwards, clutching her head. She curls up on the floor, sobbing. A thin ribbon of blood snakes out of her ear canal and winds down her earlobe.

Gasping in precious air, I drop the still wailing alarm on the floor. Tia clamps her palms over her ears.

Rage flows through me. I grab the cello, clutching its neck so tightly my knuckles turn white. I hold the sharp spike above her. I could kill her. Stop her from hurting anyone ever again.

I dry wretch. With a scream, I spin round and smash the cello against the toppled chair. The wood splinters and breaks. The remaining strings screech as they snap.

Exhaustion sweeps over me, but I force myself to stand and

stumble across to her recording equipment. I jab my fingertip against the winking red button. It's a digital system, leaving her admission of guilt trapped on the hard drive. I pull my phone out, but it's useless without a USB cable. I rifle through the chaos of objects on her desk, pushing aside scratched CDs, music scores and packets of spare cello strings.

Outside, the wail of an ambulance approaches, smothering the sound of Tia's soft crying. The siren cuts off abruptly, swiftly followed by the dull slamming of doors.

I tug open one desk drawer after another. Finally, in the bottom drawer, I find a stack of CDs and a muddled collection of wires. I sort through them, checking the ends until I find the right one. As I untwist it, I turn my attention back to Tia. She hasn't moved. She's still clutching her ears, sniffling quietly into the carpet. I can't allow myself to feel sorry for her. She's a murderer.

I plug my phone into the recording system and begin to transfer Tia's admission to it.

I go to kick the drawer shut when I glimpse the corner of a photograph, buried beneath the remaining wires. I retrieve it. Tears form a lump in my throat, blocking my breath. Three familiar faces stare out at me, happy and smiling.

Charley, Amy and Tia.

CHAPTER TWENTY-THREE

It's a dry, crisp morning. The sunlight has a golden quality to it, blanketing the whole street in a warm glow. I stand on Dad's doorstep, face to face with Kevin, who stands in awkward silence on the drive, a white plastic bag clutched in his left hand. It doesn't look heavy, but it's impossible to guess what's inside.

I clap my cold hands together. "How are you?" I can't help but stare at the fresh white bandages around his wrists.

"I'll live." He looks me in the eyes for the first time. "Thank you."

"And Tia?"

I've been expecting to hear something from the police since I gave them the recording a week ago. But even with Tia's confession in hand, they'd have a hard time proving she did anything to hurt Charley and Amy without any evidence. How could there be when she killed them with magic? I don't want to be told they're letting her go, but I have to know.

"She's been admitted to a psych facility. I'm not sure how long they'll keep her there." He sighs. "If she doesn't stop babbling about magic and angels, it's likely to be a long time."

I hope they never let her out.

"But she's okay?" I'm not sure why I care. She killed my sister.

"She has a perforated eardrum. She'll never be able to hear or play music properly again."

We both know what it means. She'll never be able to weave magic into music again. I shudder at the damage I've caused. For a few crazy moments, I wanted to be charged with assault. I intentionally hurt someone else. I deserved to be punished. But the bruises on my face and neck convinced the police my actions were self-defense. Their decision doesn't eradicate my guilt.

"You should have this," he says, thrusting the plastic bag into my hands.

I peer inside. The sunlight sparkles off shattered shards of destroyed CDs. I try to guess how many whole CDs it amounts to, but there's too many pieces.

"It's every spell we wove," he says in a low voice. "I destroyed the original files, I promise. I'm sorry for everything that happened, Kim. I hope you believe me."

"I do." I rub my arm. "But I can't forgive you. Either of you." It's not up to me to ease his guilt, but I can lessen Matthew's. I know he feels partially responsible for Charley's death. I wish he were here.

Kevin stares at the floor, his mouth scrunched into a frown. "What are you going to do now?"

I shrug. "Concentrate on my exams. I don't know beyond that." I'm not sure how I'm supposed to go back to my mundane life, after all this.

"Good luck."

I force a weak smile to my lips.

"Goodbye," he says.

I give him a small wave, watching while he wanders down the drive, towards his car. Before he reaches it, he pauses and half turns.

"I really did like you, Kim. I wish everything had been different."

"So do I." I wish he, Tia and Gage had never been a part of my life. I wish my sister was still alive. I set my jaw into a rigid line. "Goodbye, Kevin."

His mouth droops at the corners. The light in his eyes extinguishes. I watch him get into his car and drive away. My glare follows him until his car vanishes around the corner at the end of the street.

I turn to go back inside, but a flutter of movement catches my attention. Holding my breath, I swing round. Matthew is standing on the street opposite, his mottled wings fully stretched out. It's a good thing no one can see him.

I race across to him, not bothering to make sure no one is watching me.

"I was afraid I'd never see you again," I say.

"I have to go."

"Go where? Heaven?"

Amusement sparkles in his eyes and a half-smile creeps onto his lips. "Not this time. I have a vast area under my protection. I need to be where there are Baneem."

My insides turn to liquid and the certainty everything is going to be all right warms me.

"Will you come back?"

He shrugs. "Yes, if I'm needed again. I wanted to say goodbye first."

I don't want him to leave. I can't bare the uncertainty of it.

"It's not your fault," I say, sliding my fingers through his.

His brow furrows. "What isn't?"

"Charley's death. I wanted you to know I don't blame you."

"Thank you." He slips his hand free of mine. "I have to go." He smiles fully, cutting off the protests on the edge of my lips.

I can't do anything except watch as he beats his wings and rises up. The rays of the sun tangle around his body, accentuating the strong curves of his torso and arms. The light around him becomes dazzling, forcing me to shield my eyes. Then he's gone.

THE END

ABOUT THE AUTHOR

Clare Davidson is a character driven fantasy writer, teacher and mother, from the UK. Clare was born in Northampton and lived in Malaysia for four and a half years as a child, before returning to the UK to settle in Leeds with her family. Whilst attending Lancaster University, Clare met her future husband and never left. They now share their lives with their young daughter and a cranky grey cat, called Ash and an insane white kitten, called Pirate. Clare juggles family life with writing, teaching and a variety of fibre craft hobbies.

CONNECT WITH CLARE DAVIDSON

Website: http://www.claredavidson.com
Facebook: https://www.facebook.com/ClareMDavidson
Twitter: https://twitter.com/ClareMDavidson
Goodreads: http://www.goodreads.com/ClareDavidson
Mailing List: http://eepurl.com/zpjGf

ALSO BY CLARE DAVIDSON

TRINITY

Kiana longs to walk through a forest and feel grass between her toes. But she is the living embodiment of a goddess and has enemies who wish to murder her. Her death will curse the whole of Gettryne. Locked away for protection, she dreams of freedom.

Her wish comes true in the worst possible way, when her home and defenders are destroyed.

Along with an inexperienced guard and a hunted outcast, Kiana flees the ravages of battle to search for a solution to the madness that has gripped Gettryne for a thousand years. Pursued by the vicious and unrelenting Wolves, their journey will take them far beyond their limits, to a secret that will shake the world.

Available now in paperback and as an eBook.